The Tiger Cruise

By Roger Quam

Copyright © 2009 by Roger Quam

The Tiger Cruise
by Roger Quam

Printed in the United States of America

ISBN 978-1-60791-958-2

All rights reserved solely by the author. The author guarantees all contents are original and do not infringe upon the legal rights of any other person or work. No part of this book may be reproduced in any form without the permission of the author. The views expressed in this book are not necessarily those of the publisher.

www.xulonpress.com

FOREWORD

Every day, people's lives are altered by random occurrences that are never expected. An urgent phone call on a busy morning, an unexpected detour due to road construction, or arriving late for an appointment because of car trouble all set in motion events that alter the planned course of action. In turn, these events produce a chain of subsequent events—interaction with unfamiliar people, taking alternative routes, and encountering new opportunities—that change the very fabric of life itself. Some think of it as divine intervention—God's will. Sometimes these occurrences are major, resulting in even greater rearrangement of people's lives and schedules, reordering of priorities, and postponing plans. Such is the story of The Tiger Cruise.

Chapter 1

The Tiger Cruise — Day 1 — Wednesday

As the contents of the Coast Guard tugboat were being loaded onto the surfaced USS Michigan Trident Nuclear Submarine, a small fishing vessel appeared through the morning mist moving slowly toward the sub. Two people appeared to be seated and fishing in the boat, but they were looking straight ahead through binoculars. A young sailor peered at them through his binoculars and yelled out above the noise of the seawater splashing against the mammoth sub's side, "It's two women wearing baseball caps. They have fishing rods in their hands, but they're not fishing. They're just sitting there. They both have me in their sights. The boat's pilot appears to be in the cabin."

Well-armed sailors on the surface of the sub were closely watching the small fishing vessel. Their guns were loaded and ready to aim and fire. Using all of the USS Michigan's surveillance equipment, the command center personnel inside the massive vessel had zeroed in on the small fishing boat long before it had been visually spotted by the crew on the sub's topside. The comparatively tiny boat suddenly altered its course and moved closer toward the Michigan.

"Identify yourselves," shouted a sailor into his hand-held public address system. The navy chief in attendance called for everyone to be still, and all activity stopped. Everyone on top of the sub was watching and waiting quietly. The armed sailors were ready for action. The pilot of the boat cut his engine. Only the waves slapping against the huge sub and the whistling of the morning breeze were audible, allowing for clear and unencumbered communication between the two vessels.

"I'm the boat operator, Mackie Henderson, of Freddie's Deep Sea Fishing, and I have two women customers aboard," answered the man inside the cabin using the boat's PA system. The older woman hurriedly opened the door of the cabin, grabbed the microphone from the boat pilot's hand, and began to speak in a frightened tone, "My name is Virginia Johnson, and my son Jacob Johnson is aboard the Michigan. I just want to say hi and wave to him."

There was a pause while the younger woman took the microphone. "My name is Julie." She then handed the microphone back to the boat pilot, obviously unwilling to share any more information about herself.

"Stop where you are and do not come any closer," was the message from the Michigan to the fishing vessel. But Mackie had already restarted his engine, and within seconds the boat had increased its speed and was getting very close to the Michigan. The news about the women was quickly but briefly communicated to the captain inside the control room. The response was immediate.

"Do not come any closer. Hold your present location until we have submerged," relayed the radio operator. There was another short interval of conversation between the Michigan's captain and the sailor holding the communications device. Meanwhile, the Coast Guard tugboat's contents of supplies, men, and gear were being unloaded with greater speed onto the sub's topside and down the main hatch.

As the fishing boat was moving toward the sub, an explosion suddenly rang out in the water a hundred feet away. To the shock and amazement of the Michigan's crew, someone was shooting at the fishing boat! A second explosion soon followed within a shorter distance from the boat. The command and control center suddenly came alive. The explosions brought about an immediate initiation of emergency measures and procedures throughout the Michigan.

"Do not approach the sub! Keep your distance!" the sailor yelled into his PA system. It was too late.

The fishing boat quickly moved to the side of the Michigan. The two women stood up and tried to reach the top of the sub with their hands. The sailors reached down and attempted to grab onto the women's hands and to bring them onboard. Neither of the women was wearing a life jacket.

Suddenly, the older woman lost her balance, fell overboard, and slipped below the surface of the water. Without hesitation a young, lanky sailor quickly dived into the cool sea to rescue her. He took her in his right arm as she locked her arms around his neck, and they surfaced together within a few seconds. The rescuer took hold of a rope with his left hand, wrapped it around his arm, and let the onboard sailors lift the two of them onto the deck. Other sailors then brought up the younger woman. A blanket was wrapped around the older woman who had taken in some water and was coughing. She was shivering from the cold water and the chilly October air.

Mackie yelled up to the sailors on the deck, "I'm taking my boat to shore. I'm not leaving it here!" With that, he immediately turned his boat around and sped off in the direction of land. Within ten seconds the boat was at full speed heading in a southerly direction, and everyone's eyes were glued to it.

When the boat was a half-mile away, a third shot hit its target and the fishing boat disintegrated in a fiery explosion. It was then that another boat was spotted through the mist. That vessel had fired the projectile which had put an end to the fishing boat and its pilot. The situation was now critical, and the Michigan itself was in danger.

"Let's move it, sailors. We need to submerge NOW!" barked a Michigan officer who had come through the top hatch to take charge of the situation.

Within minutes all had lowered themselves down the main hatch with the two women being led away under armed guard. As soon as the hatch was closed, the Michigan began its dive below the surface. "DIVE! DIVE!" was the order heard throughout the Michigan over the PA system, and emergency measures were being put into action. Meanwhile, a radio communication had come in by satellite that an unidentified—and presumed unfriendly—foreign submarine was reported to be within ten miles of the Michigan's position. A nearby

The Tiger Cruise

U.S. fast-attack sub was on its way to intercept and, if necessary, destroy the foreign vessel.

* * * * *

In early February 2001, fifteen excited navy dads from different locations around the United States were preparing to make a trip to the state of Washington, where they would board and travel with their navy sons on the USS Michigan, one of the thirteen United States Trident Nuclear Ballistic Missile Submarines. The planned date of the trip was to be February 15, 2001. Such an event is known as a Tiger Cruise, where selected male members of the crew's family proudly share a few days with their sailor kin—a son, brother, father or grandson.

Each had been excited and anxiously anticipating the activities that would transpire during the short cruise. Other than the departure location and what to bring, little information was given to the dads in advance. They had been given a complete security check through their social security numbers provided by their naval kin onboard the sub.

Then on February 10, 2001, the U.S. Navy contacted all fifteen people with the disappointing news. The Tiger Cruise was being indefinitely postponed.

"What happened?" was the question asked by each member of the group.

"We cannot say," was the answer provided by their relatives onboard the Michigan.

The delay was precipitated by two unrelated tragedies, seven months apart, in the year 2001.

The first was a tragedy three time zones away from the West Coast of the United States. The Greenville, a fast-attack submarine demonstrating an emergency "blow" procedure near the island of Oahu in Hawaii, had an accident.

Rumors were circulated that the Greenville was engaged in an "emergency blow" during its own Tiger Cruise. Apparently, the emergency blow activator, or "chicken switch," located at the ballast control panel in the sub's attack center was flipped. It can be activated only by the chief of the watch. Exactly who or what caused the blow to take place was never released.

A Japanese fishing boat, the Ehime Maru, was on the surface when the Greenville surfaced and slammed into it, breaking it into two pieces. The tragic accident caused nine Japanese fishermen to drop to their deaths in two thousand feet of water. As a result, investigations were initiated by both of the governments involved, and all Tiger Cruises involving the U.S. Navy were immediately placed on hold until the uproar had subsided.

Fast forward seven months—to September 11, 2001. Hijacked commercial airliners smashed into the World Trade Towers in New York City, the Pentagon in Washington, D.C., and an open field in Pennsylvania. This act of terrorism affected the activities of most people in the United States. The result was greatly heightened terrorist awareness and increased security in all international travel.

The USS Michigan Tiger Cruise dads continued their regular daily lives, and many of them wondered if the rendezvous with their sons on the Michigan would ever take place. A second chance at this "once in a lifetime trip" might never occur while their sons were still on the sub or even in the navy. The travel and overnight bags were set aside, if not totally unpacked, by the dads.

Finally, in early September 2003, calls were made around the country, and the fifteen Tiger Cruise candidates once again planned for the journey to the state of Washington to embark on their trip of a lifetime. The interrupted excitement resumed with even greater intensity.

The fifteen invited guests of the Michigan crew finally met in a parking lot at the Bangor, Washington, submarine base. As they arrived, they were at first quiet and reserved, not knowing what to expect next. The ice was finally broken when one of the dads asked another dad, "How long has it been since you've seen your boy?"

"Last Christmas," was the answer.

Within minutes, everyone was engaged in conversations about their homes, families, jobs, and the trip they were about to take. The morning was dreary and foggy—typical of the weather in western Washington next to the Puget Sound.

The Tiger Cruise

Soon two white buses drove into the parking lot and stopped. Naval officers with clipboards under their arms and the bus drivers exited their buses simultaneously. The officers began to read off the names of the crew. One by one, they picked up their gear and entered one of the two buses as instructed. The seats were close together and the aisles narrow. There was only enough room for one person in each seat. The gear was piled onto the available empty seats, some of it protruding into the aisle, which made maneuvering within the bus most difficult.

After an hour-long ride in the cramped bus to the John Wayne Marina in Sequim, Washington, the Tiger Crew disembarked with all their gear and began a wait on the dock, as instructed by one of the naval officers. The other officer walked onto the dock and said, "Welcome, Tiger Crew, to the U.S. Navy. Here are the plans: We are waiting for a Coast Guard boat to arrive and take us out to the sub. It's a half-hour ride, and hopefully we'll all be able to board with only one trip. I'm not sure of the size of the boat we're getting. We have at least an hour wait here, so if you'd like to go to the café and get some breakfast, feel free to do so. Keep close, however. We don't want to leave any of you. Neither does your family member onboard the Michigan."

Some of the crew set their gear down on the dock and made their way to the small restaurant to grab a bite to eat. A few climbed to the top floor gift shop, while others went for a stroll around the marina grounds. The remainder of the Tiger Crew sat down on their bags or on the nearby benches and continued getting acquainted with each other.

Three of the men seated on the dock soon found a common topic to discuss and one that was very much on their minds—their ex-wives' lawyers.

"I think there is going to be a special place in hell for those scum bag lawyers—maybe a place where they'll have to marry our ex-wives," one of the men said.

"Hey! Don't laugh! My ex did marry that scum bag!" voiced another dad.

"You're kidding! How'd that happen?" asked the third dad.

The Tiger Cruise

"They're from the same pod on the vine—from hell. It's a long story and I will fill you in on the sordid details when we have more time," was the answer.

In an hour, the navy dads once again gathered as they saw and heard the Coast Guard tugboat. Everyone watched as it arrived and maneuvered against the dock. They loaded the gear and themselves onto the small craft, and the boat soon became quite crowded. Each man sat wherever he could find room. There was also increased anticipation of what was about to take place.

"Some of you and your gear will need to go below in order for everything to fit," one of the officers shouted out. "We have a large amount of food to bring out to the sub. You men will be eating much of it in the next two days, so we don't want to leave any of it." One of the dads had received permission from the captain of the Michigan to bring onboard nine quarts of homemade salsa for the crew.

After the men, gear and food were on the boat, they began the journey out toward the open waters of the Strait of Juan de Fuca.

The air was hazy and cool. Those not inside the boat's cabin were doused by the spray mist that the splashing seawater produced when colliding with the boat's side. Those inside the cabin attempted to make conversation above the roar of the boat's deafening engine, but that soon became futile.

As the boat moved away from land, the long outline of a huge sub soon began to emerge on the misty horizon. One of the dads first spotted it with his binoculars through the morning fog. The Tiger Crew became quiet. Stories and movies of submarines began to reappear in the minds of the men. The enormous size of the mammoth sub no longer was a mere statistic—it was real! The sub was 566 feet long and forty-two feet in diameter. Only a fraction of those dimensions was visible above the water line, and the sub was the only object visible above the horizon. The personnel on the Michigan consisted of fourteen officers, eighteen chief petty officers, and 122 enlisted sailors—totaling 154 men.

The Coast Guard boat soon arrived at the surfaced Michigan. Everyone joined in to unload the gear. The men could hardly contain their excitement. The Tiger Cruise aboard the USS Michigan had finally begun!

The Tiger Cruise

****

The two women were escorted to Captain Jasper Wagner's quarters for a meeting. They stopped at a bathroom long enough for Virginia to change into some dry navy clothes provided by one of the chiefs. One of the sailors wrapped a blanket around her to provide additional warmth. The captain had come from the control room and had just started an emergency meeting with some of his chiefs. He stopped the meeting and turned to the women standing outside of the narrow doorway. All of the chiefs stood up until the women had entered and had been seated.

Captain Wagner remained standing and said, "I'm not sure what is going on with you two, so you'll need to be secured until further notice. I know you gave us your names while you were still on the fishing boat, but with all the commotion we didn't ... What are your names again?"

"I'm Virginia Johnson," the older woman answered back with a half smile on her face.

"Ginger? I didn't recognize you! What are you doing here?" Captain Wagner briefly glanced out to the hall attempting perchance to see his retired naval friend Chief Warren Johnson, who was Ginger's ex-husband. Jasper Wagner and Warren Johnson had served together for three years aboard the fast-attack submarine, the USS Indianapolis. Warren was aboard the Michigan as a Tiger Crew member, invited by his navy son Jake.

"I knew the Michigan was going to be out here, and I wanted to at least wave to my son Jacob," she answered. "It's been a long time since I've seen him."

The captain glanced at the taller and younger woman, and then asked Ginger, "Did you know that Warren was going to be one of the Tiger Crew?"

"Yes, I did," Ginger answered.

The captain turned back to the younger woman. "What's your story?"

"My name is Julie Furniture. I just met Ginger two nights ago after a concert near Seattle. She invited me to come with her on the fishing boat to see the Michigan. I had never seen an actual submarine, but I've been interested in them for a long time. Both of us hired the fishing boat operator to take us out to see the sub. We even tried some fishing while we were waiting."

The captain was quiet for a few seconds and then spoke again. "Do either of you ladies have any idea what all of that shooting was about between those boats on the surface?"

Julie answered, "I'm going to guess here, but I suspect that drugs were involved. I overheard Mackie talking to someone on his cell phone about it. They were yelling at each other, and Mackie acted very scared. I couldn't believe he would have that kind of a conversation in front of two customers he'd never met before. I was actually getting scared about being anywhere near that man."

The captain broke in and said, "I need to continue my meeting here with my chiefs, but I'll see you later. Meanwhile, we'll need to provide an escort for you until further notice. We normally would call them guards, but we will call them escorts in your case. We need to get official emergency security clearance for each of you ladies. If you could just stay in the mess hall for a short while, I'll have my housing chief find some quarters for you. We will also find a convenient bathroom facility for you girls. You'll need an escort with you at all times. We may trust you girls, but not so much the boys. Also, the areas that you will have access to will be limited, at least until we have a security clearance on you."

The women left the captain's quarters and were escorted to the mess hall. The housing chief and some of the Michigan's crew hurriedly emptied a storage room of its contents, cleaned it thoroughly, set up two small cots with bedding, and supplied other necessities on a small table. The room was close to the Michigan's mess hall, The Great Lakes Café, and away from the sailors' sleeping quarters.

The Tiger Crew members were given beds by the nuclear silos. They were three tiers high with a ladder to aid in climbing into them. Bedding was provided by the housing chief, and the location of the bathroom facilities was shown to the new guests.

The entire Tiger Crew spent the afternoon in the mess hall, which was located on the Michigan's first level. A sign over the main door read, "Welcome to the Great Lakes Café." On a wall inside the café was another sign which read, "This is not your mother's kitchen, and your mother is not onboard to keep it clean. That is your job."

The tables were covered with plastic red-and-white-checkered tablecloths, and a large American flag hung on the wall at the opposite end of the serving line. There was the ever-popular salad bar down the middle, and the coffee and soft drinks table was against the wall. The mess hall was the gathering place for all of ship's personnel, even the command. It was the place where the Michigan's least experienced sailor could sit down by the commander and talk about football or submarines. It was a happy room—most of the time.

The high state of alert was still the order of the day, but the unexpected situation was a blessing—it allowed the Tiger Crew to get to know more about each other from the start.

Since the two women were not able to bring onto the sub any of their personal items, the supply chief was assigned to do what he could. Most normal hygiene items were no problem. The clothing was another matter. The only option was to use regular navy uniforms, including boots and caps. The girls didn't object, mainly because they had no other choice. They did have what they wore when they came on the sub, which they would have to wear once the sub surfaced.

As they came into the mess hall with their navy attire, a spontaneous round of applause was their vote of confidence and acceptance. The ladies found this attitude a pleasant change from the disruption and urgency a few hours earlier.

Julie and Ginger sat by themselves at lunch. The mess hall was busy, and the crowded room prevented the women from observing most of the sailors. Finally, many of the crew cleared out, and they spotted the sailor who had rescued Ginger. Having just obtained his lunch, he found an empty chair at their table and joined them.

"What is your name, young man?" Ginger asked the tall and handsome young sailor.

"My name is David Cordell, ma'am," he answered.

"I want to thank you for rescuing me this morning," Ginger said with sincerity and gratitude.

"You are welcome, ma'am," he responded, "but I was only doing my job and what any of these sailors would have done. That's what we were trained to do—rescue pretty ladies from the ocean. Excuse me for a moment." David became quiet. He bowed his head and prayed silently over his meal. When his praying was finished, he lifted his head and opened his eyes. Julie waited until he was looking at her before she rolled her eyes, doing it purposely for him to see. Seemingly surprised, David looked at Ginger, who smiled back at him. She had observed the entire incident. David returned her smile with one of his, as if to say, "you and I must be on the same team."

Julie excused herself and walked over to the salad bar to add to her plate. David watched her as she walked. She was just a little shorter than his height, but still tall—probably five foot, ten inches, he calculated in his mind. David was six foot, one inch tall. He looked closer as she walked. She was very well proportioned with long legs, arms, and fingers. Her fingers were especially long. Her long, black hair was tied up and sitting on top of her head. Julie's facial features made her appearance look like she could be on the cover of any woman's magazine on the newsstand. She was very attractive and graceful. David was captivated with her beauty and kept his eyes on her as she approached her chair.

"Do you have a dad on this Tiger Cruise?" Ginger asked David.

"No, ma'am ... my dad couldn't make it," David answered, still admiring Julie as she returned to the table and sat down.

David commenced eating his meal while Ginger and Julie continued to talk. Soon Ginger's son Jake walked up to the table. She stood up and gave him a hug. "This is a surprise, Mom. I never expected to see you—much less seeing you come onboard in this manner," Jake said. The young sailor sat down on the empty seat next to his mother.

David finished his meal, gathered his dishes and tableware, and deposited them at the dishwashing window. As he was leaving the mess hall, he came face to face with Julie, who was also leaving with her escort. Neither of them said anything as their eyes met momentarily. In that short time, David memorized her face. Something told him that this would not be the last time they would meet.

The Tiger Cruise

All of the Tiger Cruise members were called for a meeting in the dining room after the evening meal. As soon as they had gathered, Captain Wagner walked in and made a statement.

"Two things: First, we'll meet here in the morning at 0900, or right after breakfast, for our orientation, which was postponed from this afternoon. Secondly, I don't have much I can tell you about what's happening in our current emergency crisis, but I will open it up for a few questions."

One of the Tiger Crew eagerly asked, "Captain Wagner, what is the status of the reported foreign submarine close by us?"

The captain looked down at his clipboard for a moment, then looked back at the Tiger Crew member and answered, "It is true that an unidentified submarine is in our vicinity. Who is in control of the sub is not yet known, and no group or country has claimed ownership."

"When will we be able to contact our families at home about our situation?" another asked.

"At this time, my guess is the Navy is contacting your wives and families with word that you are safe. That is all we are telling them. At some point and when it is safe, we will set up a secured satellite phone for each of you to call and talk to your family. There will be certain restrictions as to what you may tell them, however."

"How long will we be submerged?" was the next question by someone in back of the room.

"Good question ... and one that we don't know the answer to. I'm afraid, gentlemen, that I must conclude this meeting to attend to other pressing matters. See you in the morning."

Very shortly after 11:00 p.m., there was a sudden loud noise from inside one of the bathrooms. Since they were very close to the bathrooms, the members of the Tiger Crew who were already asleep were awakened with a jolt! The area was quickly sealed off with only Michigan crew members being permitted to investigate. The Tiger Crew gathered out in the hall, and one of them guessed that the explosion may have come from the nuclear engine room. The rumor spread like wild fire. Although it was not the case, the fear of radiation leakage was on the mind of each man in the gathered group.

The Tiger Cruise

All of the Tiger Crew got dressed and hurried to the mess hall for coffee and conversation. The first day of the Tiger Cruise had ended with both excitement and fear on everyone's mind. The subject of discussion at the coffee sessions had turned from family and careers to surviving on a nuclear submarine lost somewhere in the ocean waters off the coast of Washington. Now there was cause to worry not only about a foreign submarine creeping into proximity of the Michigan, but also about the unknown source of an engine room explosion and the damage it may have inflicted. What else could go wrong on this Tiger Cruise?

David lay in his bunk thinking about Julie. He had been captivated by her beauty as never before in his young life. Their meeting at lunch did not bode well for David, but he hoped he would have a chance to formally meet her within a day or two. Then again, so did all of the other young sailors on the Michigan. That same subject was also of concern to the captain, officers, and the chiefs. They had never had to deal with women on their submarine before.

Chapter 2

The Tiger Cruise—Day 2—Thursday

At the start of the second day, the command of the USS Michigan was busy tracking the yet-unconfirmed enemy submarine and its country of origin. Gathered around the sonar desk were Captain Wagner, the chief of the boat, the lieutenant commander, the ship's navigator, and the communications officer. Because of the potential national security implications, there was no communication to or from the outside world by the Michigan. The world was filled with news stories of a fishing boat being blown up by another boat using high-powered guns and subsequently causing a United States submarine to hide deep in the ocean. Another story told about a foreign naval vessel being involved. Some news stories reported it as a lost nuclear submarine. What really was selling was the news of two women being rescued by the sailors of the Michigan and being hidden on the sub. The Navy was busy attempting to calm the families of all onboard and to feed the frenzied news media just the right amount of correct information.

* * * * *

The entire Tiger Crew couldn't believe the fantastic food they had been served so far on their journey. Their sons had talked about it and the family members most often thought that they were joking. They weren't, and the dads were finding that out first hand. A few

The Tiger Cruise

of these dads were slightly overweight, and they became alarmed as they thought about the pounds they could add to their waistlines if the crisis did not come to an end soon.

David was surprised when one of the chiefs came to him while he was shaving in the bathroom. "David," the chief said, "Captain Wagner has requested that you attend the Tiger Crew orientation at 0900 in the mess hall. The older woman aboard the sub, who you fished out of the water yesterday, has requested that you be there as her guest."

"Yes, sir," David replied after quickly putting his shaver down and saluting the chief. *Maybe this is where I'll get to meet Julie,* he thought. "Sir, did the younger woman say anything about my being present at the meeting?"

"Nothing was said to me about her," the chief answered with a puzzled look.

After breakfast, Captain Wagner announced on the intercom that all Tiger Crew members were to meet in the mess hall. Some of the crew arrived early and helped set up two rows of chairs in a semi-circle. The captain asked everyone to be seated with their naval kin sitting directly behind them. This included the two women aboard. David took the seat behind Ginger. No one sat behind Julie, and it gave David a great view of her.

Captain Wagner stood before the group and said, "My name is Jasper Wagner. I am the commander of the USS Michigan Trident Nuclear Submarine, but you may call me 'Captain.' Some of the sailors on this sub call me Skipper Wagner. Please feel free to talk to me at any time, except when I am in a meeting with my officers or chiefs. I may even sit with you and drink some of our delicious flavored coffee on occasion here in the Great Lakes Café.

"This orientation session should have been held yesterday as soon as you boarded the Michigan. However, we seemed to have had a slight interruption and delay. Rather, we needed to get going real fast." The gathered group produced a brief and low-volume chuckle. The Captain once again became serious and continued, "We are on the highest alert; therefore, security is of utmost importance. I am

22

up to my neck with emergency meetings, as I'm sure you all understand. So at this time, I will turn this session over to one of my able chiefs, Bernard Thornbloom."

Captain Wagner started to exit the room but turned around before he got to the door and said, "Oh, one other thing ... The explosion you heard last night came from one of the bathrooms. It seems that something was flushed down the toilet and trapped some gas. To make matters worse, someone threw a lighted match in just the right place and ... Boom! Be careful to not flush anything but 'you know what' down the toilet, and only smoke in the smoking room. Thank you."

There was a sudden burst of laughter from the Tiger Crew—not only from the funny story, but also from the sense of relief to all of them.

Chief Thornbloom was a medium-sized, slender-built, balding middle-aged sailor. He was well-dressed in his navy uniform with his black shoes shined to perfection. He spoke in a deep, raspy voice—totally unexpected from someone with his lean build.

"Hello, and welcome aboard the USS Michigan. I trust your stay will be a pleasant one and your journey even more exciting than your arrival ... if that is even remotely possible. This cruise was only supposed to last two days, but it is entirely possible now that we may be submerged for much longer. We do have about two weeks of food in storage aboard the sub. That is unless you people eat like sailors."

The Tiger Crew again gave a quiet laugh.

"Here are some things you need to know for the safety of the sub, the crew, and, of course, yourselves. Be sure to 'stand fast and clear' of all passageways and operating crews, especially during an emergency. And do not interfere with anyone's work." He then showed the gathered crew how to use the emergency breathing masks, should an emergency require their usage.

"The instructions in the General Information section of the orientation booklet, which is being passed out to you as I speak, are very clear on what to do and what not to do. Do not operate any equipment or switches, position any valves, or enter any posted area without prior approval. And, of course, certain rooms are off limits— the radio room, sonar room, sonar equipment room, data processing

The Tiger Cruise

room, missile control center, and the engine room. Otherwise you are free to roam around the sub. Just be careful not to touch what you should not touch."

Each member of the Tiger Crew was given a booklet titled *Welcome Aboard*. In the sixteen-page booklet were the statistical data of the Michigan, a photo of the captain and his biography, and a history of various seagoing vessels that had the name "Michigan." There was also some general information—a brief description of how a nuclear sub is powered and various other pertinent facts.

"I would like to have each of you introduce yourselves and your sailor son, brother, nephew, or grandson to the rest of the Tiger Crew; and then tell us about yourself, your family, your work, your interests, etcetera. I would also ask you to tell something unique about yourself. We have at least thirty minutes for this part of the orientation session. Then we'll go over some ground rules about our cruise, what we have scheduled for you, and a few minutes for questions and answers.

"Now for the bad news. I need to inform you that because of our high alert status, each of you may be asked to perform some duties on the Michigan during the duration of our cruise. This will greatly facilitate our maintenance and watch schedule. I am asking each of you to fill out a brief information sheet to determine what work experience you have, what you are good at doing, what you like to do, etcetera. We'll hire you into the naval service as a civilian, and you'll earn a sailor's basic wage plus sea pay. Each of you will receive a special discharge certificate when you leave the sub. This work detail will last only until the current crisis is over. Also, the Navy will be contacting your family at home and informing them of your status.

"I cannot tell you much about what is going on around us in the Pacific waters, and we need to maintain our silence. Be prepared to be on the Michigan for an indeterminate amount of time. We'll need to surface sometime or we'll run out of food. You'd be amazed what these sailors can put away into their stomachs in a short period of time. Maybe you already know that about your sons." The men laughed in agreement.

The Tiger Crew was visibly worried about the crisis they were under, and this exercise would provide a brief respite from their

The Tiger Cruise

anxiety. Most of them had obligations at home and family that were more than likely worried about them.

The group began to be more at ease and ready to take turns introducing themselves. They were thinking of some details about themselves and their lives. The first to speak was the dad who was sitting directly to the left of Chief Thornbloom. The chief motioned to the dad to begin.

"Hi, everybody! My name is Oscar Lindquist, and I am fifty-seven years of age. My son Sander, behind me, is one of four children that my wife and I have. Sandy is the oldest. I live in the town of Lindstrom, Minnesota—an area that was settled by Swedish immigrants in the late 1800s. My grandfather came from Sweden and settled on 160 acres given to him by the then-current United States administration. Grandpa broke the sod, dug out the stones and tree roots, farmed the land, and then gave it to my father, who in turn gave it to me. I will someday pass the land on to one of my children—that is if one of them wants it. What is interesting about both Sander and me is that we are full Swede—not a drop of Norwegian blood in us. A unique thing about me is that I have an extra thumb on my left hand. I have often thought of having it sawed off, but I never got around to it. Ask me sometime and I will show it to you." At that point, Oscar stopped talking and turned to the Tiger Crew member on his left.

"I guess I'm next. My name is Frederick Quanto, and I'm sixty years old. My son Daniel is one of the sailors on this submarine. I'm happy to be here and waited for this trip for several months ... which, as you know, stretched into years. I guess we all have been waiting.

"I am from Sloan, Iowa, just a short drive south of Sioux City, right off Interstate 29. After an eight-year stretch in the Air Force, I became a rural mail carrier for thirty years before retiring. Now I live in a small house on the edge of Sloan and have a hobby farm. My wife and I grow veggies and flowers. She keeps busy making quilts. Both of us sell some of our produce, quilts and flowers at the Farmer's Market in Sioux City on Saturdays in the spring, summer, and fall. I hope I'll be able to chat with all of you at some time during this cruise, and maybe I'll share some good recipes for chili that I have formulated. Next? ... Oh, I almost forgot. Two unique

The Tiger Cruise

things about me. I was born on February 29, Leap Year, and I'm a ventriloquist."

The first two introductions went well and seemed to put the group at ease. The relaxed atmosphere was a stark change from how the cruise had started out. The introductions continued.

"As you can tell by my navy cap, I was once a naval chief. I'm Warren Johnson, age fifty-four, and behind me is my son Jake Johnson ... or as his mother loves to call him, Jacob. Sadly to say, Jake's mother and I were divorced when he was a teenager. My ex-wife, Virginia, is the older of the two ladies who are now in our presence. I hope that all of you have a chance to meet her during the cruise. Jake got all of his good features from his mother."

At that point Warren stopped and looked down, trying to regain control of his emotions and stop his voice from breaking. Ginger teared up. It was difficult for him to go on; but after an awkward ten seconds, he resumed his introduction.

"After serving twenty years in the navy, part of that time with the captain of this sub, I retired. I now work part-time as a business consultant and spend much of my spare time fishing on Lake Huron. My home is in Flint, Michigan. Whenever Jake comes home, we try to fish for the big lunkers or do some deer hunting. I guess I'm trying to make up for lost time with my boy. Unfortunately, a military career sometimes interferes with raising a family. I regret this and would like to go back and live it over again. But you don't want to hear about that part of my life." There was a short pause.

"What's unique about you, Dad?" Jake asked.

"I play the harmonica and sing at the same time. Who's next?" With that Warren turned to the dad on his left.

"I guess that would be me. Alex Perkins is my name and I'm from Boise, Idaho. My age is sixty as of today. Son Duane is sitting behind me. Maybe he can tell you more about me." Alex stopped abruptly and waited for his son to continue. Then Alex suddenly reached down, picked up a tiny scrap of paper off of the floor, hurriedly removed his handkerchief from his back pocket, and proceeded to vigorously wipe the seat of his chair that was exposed between his widely spread legs. He seemed uncomfortable speaking.

The Tiger Cruise

It was apparent that his son Duane was not expecting this to happen, but he took over.

"My dad was a high school social studies teacher for about twenty years when he had a nervous breakdown. He is now disabled. The breakdown caused him to develop a nervous condition known as obsessive-compulsive disorder, or OCD. I think it is well that you all know about my father's condition from the start so you'll understand it when you see him." Duane stopped at that point and patted his dad on the shoulders with both hands. Then he continued.

"Unfortunately, my mom didn't understand or accept my dad's condition following his breakdown, so she divorced him. Dad does take some medication for his condition, but they tell us the nervous behavior that he displays cannot be totally suppressed or cured. Maybe doctors will find a medicine to cure it someday.

"People routinely leave their houses every day, get into their cars and drive off. But if those same people happen to have OCD, it may take them several hours just to get out of the house. They keep switching the lights on and off fearing that they don't have the lights completely off. Or they may rearrange a table of items over and over again. I hope you will engage my dad in your activities and help him if he gets hung up."

The room was completely quiet for a moment, with only sounds coming from the submarine's ventilation system and dishes rattling in the kitchen. The informal thirty minutes was turning into a "tell-all" session. Captain Thornbloom looked over to where two other chiefs were sitting and gave them a facial expression that said, "Can we experience any more challenges on this trip?" All eyes shifted from Alex to the next Tiger Crew member.

"I'm next. My name is Joseph 'Joe' Rosenberg, age eighty, which probably qualifies me as being the oldest Tiger aboard the Michigan. Behind me is my grandson Itzak Rosenberg. I am from Brooklyn, New York, where I am retired. Itzak's grandmother passed on a few years ago. I was born and raised in Germany and moved to Brooklyn when Nazi Germany became too hot for us Jews to exist. The extended families that we left behind were all killed—or rather murdered—either in the concentration camps or during the journey to them. When my parents and I moved to Brooklyn, I studied

English day and night. I became a piano player in a dance band, took a turn at conducting a symphony orchestra, and finally went to college and became a history professor. I now spend much of my time working as a volunteer at a Jewish nursing home as a cook. My unique feature is that I have a bird that sings Elvis Presley songs. I have to teach the songs to him, of course. Next!"

Everyone seemed to be attentive and enjoying the brief introductions.

"I'm Max Schroeder, age fifty-two, and the father of Gerald 'Jerry' Schroeder. My father was born in Germany, was in Hitler's army, and, sad to say, was quite cruel to Mr. Rosenberg's people. Fortunately, my father was wounded and taken prisoner. I say fortunately, because he was sent to a POW camp in America and ended up settling in Georgia rather then returning to Germany when the war ended. If he had not been captured, my father may have not made it to the end of the war alive. Consequently, I may not have been born."

Max reached out his hand and took Joe Rosenberg's hand, shook it, then continued his introduction. "I live in Marietta, Georgia, where I work as a salesman of grave stones—I call them memorials—and coffins. People are dying to do business with me! I am divorced also. That's another complete story. Maybe I'll share it during a coffee session with some of you. My unique feature is that my ex-wife's lawyer is now married to my ex-wife."

Max sat down and the man next to him stood up.

"I'm Julian Chesney, age forty-six, father of Wayne, my sailor son. My current home is in Reston, Virginia, from where I commute to work in Washington, DC. I am an accountant in the government with most of my work being on my computer. I play tennis and at one time had an aspiration of playing in the Olympics. My wife's name is Betty, and she and I have four other children. What is my unique feature? Would you believe I was once a lighthouse operator?" He turned and motioned to the dad on his left, the only African-American Tiger father on the cruise.

"I'm William 'Bill' Wallace, age fifty. My son, William Junior, is sitting behind me. I am the great-grandson of a slave who lived in Kentucky. After the Civil War, great-granddaddy worked on the farm and eventually bought it from his former master. It has been passed down to me, and someday I hope to pass it on to one of my children. I spend much of my spare time restoring old farm machinery and cars. If any of you ever get to Louisville, I'll let you take one of my cars for a spin on an old country road."

Joe Rosenberg interrupted him and asked, "What kinds of cars have you restored?"

Bill Wallace quickly answered, "I have restored five or six Model As, a couple of Model Ts, a 1928 Buick Roadmaster, a Maxwell, and an Overland. Some of you may have never heard of those old cars."

The man to the left of Bill Wallace stood up and said, "My name is Elmer Garrick and I am fifty-one years old. My son Scott is sitting behind me. I've lived in Minot, North Dakota, my entire life. I have worked as a carpenter since I was twenty-eight years old, after serving in the navy for eight years. I am married to a woman I met while serving in the navy."

Frederick Quanto interrupted Elmer and said, "I don't believe you when you say you're from Minot. Prove it by telling us what the sign says as you enter the Chamber of Commerce building in Minot."

Elmer immediately shot back, "Why Not, Minot!"

"That is correct!" Frederick confirmed.

"Where did you learn that?" asked Elmer.

"I was stationed at the Minot air base when I was in the service," he responded.

Elmer continued his introduction. "I hope we can have a good time on this cruise, considering our current situation and not knowing when we will surface again. My unique feature is that I collect hymnals and old railroad spikes. Not very exciting, but it's fun. Next Tiger."

"George Tedson is my name. I am from Richardson, Texas. I'm twenty-four years old and my twin brother, James—sitting behind me—is a sailor on this sub. Since our parents were killed in an auto accident fifteen years ago, James is the only family I have. Our grandparents raised us, but they are both gone now, also. I'm single and work as a chemist for an oil company in Texas. Next!"

Each Tiger Crew member had settled into the routine of saying, "Next!" to signify when he had finished with his introduction.

The Tiger Cruise

Julie quickly focused her attention on George the moment he mentioned he was single. David noticed Julie's attention.

"I'm probably the only Hawaiian Tiger Crew member on board. Gustav Minter is my name, age sixty-six, and I am part Japanese and part German. My grandson Brad is sitting behind me. I now live in Aiea, Hawaii, which is a suburb of Honolulu. I am married to a Japanese woman whom I met when I was stationed at Pearl in 1971. I have a very unique heritage—both of my grandparents fought against the United States during the Second World War. My one granddad was in the German Navy and the other fought with the Japanese Navy. Unfortunately, they were both killed in action. I never knew my grandfathers. My grandmothers were war brides.

"My wife and I are both retired from the restaurant business and now spend our days gardening and relaxing on the edge of Honolulu. I am able to recite the 'Pledge of Allegiance' backwards, in three languages—English, Japanese, and German. That's all I have to tell you." There was a brief pause signaling to the next Tiger Crew member that it was his turn.

"Let me add to the mix of nationalities on this submarine. I am a Spanish-American. I'm Fernando Perez, age fifty-seven, and my son is Carlos Perez. I live in San Antonio, Texas. I work as a detective in the police department, play golf, enjoy jazz, and do some traveling. On weekends I play in a five-piece Dixieland jazz band. It was while playing in a band as a young man that I met my wife, Maria. Carlos's mother and I are now divorced. However, both of our divorce lawyers have fallen in love with each other and were recently married. My uniqueness is that I love history—any kind of history." He turned to the dad on his left. "Next!"

"Well, let's add another ethnicity to our little group. How about a Native American? More than that, would you believe that I am three-quarters Native American and one-quarter Norwegian? A lethal combination! I'm Jimmy Runsaway Olson, age seventy, and my grandson Dennis "Geronimo" Olson is right behind me. I'm a retired farmer from Plainfield, Wisconsin, and also have some notoriety in my family. My great-grandfather was a child in Montana and lived only a short distance from where Custer was killed. My wife died of cancer about ten years ago.

"Where did you get your name, Runsaway?" Fernando asked.

"I'm not telling, otherwise you'd think I and my family are cowards ... which we're not. Maybe I'll give you the full story some afternoon over coffee." He turned his head to the left and nodded to the next Tiger Crew member.

"Would you believe I'm Joseph 'Joey' Wagner, age twenty-one? My father is Jasper Wagner, the captain of the Michigan. I've completed two years of college in Tennessee. Right now I am taking a few months off to determine which way to go. I was a rebellious teenager, according to my mom and dad. I now realize that they were right and I am trying to rebuild a relationship with my dad. I guess my notoriety is that I was once attacked by a pit bull and lived to tell about it."

"What happened?" Jake Johnson asked.

"I was lucky. I ducked just as the dog was about to grab my throat, and he flew into the swimming pool. I received only a few claw marks, but otherwise I am okay. The dog belonged to the neighbor, and my dad got his gun and shot the dog in the pool. We had to drain the pool and clean it. Have any of you heard your captain, my father, tell that story?"

"Why don't you join the navy?" David asked him.

"Maybe I should," was Joey's quick answer. "I'm giving it some serious thought. Next!"

"I'm David 'Dave' Simmons, age forty-nine, and I am here on the Michigan submarine as a Tiger Crew member at the invitation of my nephew Mark Simmons. I am a medical doctor and have been divorced for five years. I live in Cleveland, Ohio."

"What kind of a doctor are you?" Oscar Lindquist asked.

"I am a neurosurgeon," Dave answered.

"Can you help me with a brain transplant?" asked Jimmy Runsaway to the laughter of the group.

"Only if we can find a donor," was Dave's quick answer, which elicited even more laughter.

There was a short break in the introductions as the cooks brought in a large tray of goodies. Everyone took a large, still-warm cookie as the tray was passed around. Loose nuts and chocolate chip smears were on the wax-paper-covered tray. Coffee and water cups were filled and passed around the semicircle of chairs. Once the treats had been distributed, the proceedings continued.

"I am Brian Denver, from Poughkeepsie, New York, age fifty-three, and I am here with my son Matthew 'Matt' Denver. My occupation is a truck driver, and yes, I love the music of Johnny Cash. I have a complete collection of his CDs in my truck. I am also divorced, which is par for truck drivers. Truck drivers seemed to have a problem with staying married. Who's next?"

"What's unique about you?" someone yelled out.

"I raise Norwegian Fjord horses on a small ranch outside of Poughkeepsie." He paused and looked at the next dad.

"I guess I'm the last to introduce myself. I'm Charles 'Chuck' Madsen, age forty-five. Jeremy is my son. I'm a stockbroker in Golden, Colorado, where my wife and I also operate The Wild Thing Bed and Breakfast. I was one of those unlucky souls who lost a bundle in the stock market crash in the late 1980s. That's about all I have to tell you, other than I really don't care to engage in too much 'shop talk' about investments on this cruise. I am on a vacation."

Chief Thornbloom sensed that the crew could use a break and some coffee refills. He stood up and announced, "Let's take a coffee and bathroom break before we ask the girls to tell us their story."

David quietly sat by himself through the ten-minute break. He wanted to formally meet and talk to Julie, but he decided to let her make the first move. She was ignoring him for reasons even she did not know. Maybe Ginger would at some point formally introduce the two of them. Meanwhile, in a few minutes he would find out more about Julie. David was anxiously waiting.

Chapter 3

The Tiger Crew gathered once again and was ready to continue. Chief Thornbloom stood up, cleared his throat, and began the remainder of the Tiger Crew introductory session. "We next need to let our two female cruise members introduce themselves. They were not part of the invited crew, but due to circumstances beyond anyone's control, they are now aboard. Once they had been declared secure and harmless, we decided to have them be part of this year's Michigan Tiger Cruise. Go ahead, girls," he said as he nodded to the older of the two women.

Virginia stood and looked around at the group, then she took a deep breath and said, "My name is Virginia Johnson, but everyone calls me Ginger. My son Jacob Johnson, sitting behind his father, still calls me Mom. I'm not telling you my age, but it's between forty-six and forty-eight ... and don't let that leave this room! And, yes, I am the ex-wife of Warren Johnson, a former navel chief. He is the guest of my son on this cruise."

She stopped momentarily and looked across the semi-circle of chairs to where Chief Johnson was sitting looking down at the floor. Noticing the pause, he looked up and saw her looking directly at him. They locked eyes intently, and then she continued with her introduction.

"You're probably wondering why I am on the Michigan. Well, I'll tell you. It's because the captain was merciful enough to allow me to come aboard. I owe my life to the captain and to a tall, handsome, lanky sailor who fished me out of the cold water. I just met sailor David Cordell yesterday at lunch, and I requested his presence here this morning so I could publicly thank him." She looked

The Tiger Cruise

at David sitting behind her, then turned her head toward Julie, who was sitting next to her.

Ginger continued, "Many of you saw what happened when our boat driver took off; both he and his boat were blown up. Julie and I could have both been on that boat and become food for the sharks. Why he was being targeted, I have no idea. I trust the authorities are investigating.

"Julie and I met each other after a piano concert a few nights ago. We met again just yesterday morning at Freddie's Deep Sea Fishing, and I invited her to come with me. We both wanted to have a look at the Michigan and maybe wave or say hi to the sailors. I had no idea that we would be in the center of this big of a crisis.

"I've lived in Florida for the past few years teaching high school literature. I've also done some volunteer work at an ESL center. Right now I am on leave from my teaching job. Exactly what my future plans are I still don't know." She paused for a few seconds. "Julie, you're next." She patted the woman next to her on the knee as she took her seat. Julie had no one sitting behind her.

Julie's beauty and physical appearance held most of those gathered in the mess hall in a state of amazement. This tall young woman standing in the exact middle of the Great Lakes Café was very attractive. She wore a pair of black slacks and a light-blue long-sleeved shirt—the same outfit she had on when she boarded the sub. She was also wearing a USS Michigan navy cap with scrambled eggs on the brim—the same cap that the captain usually wore. Under her hat she had her long black hair tied up. Her shoes were black with a silver buckle. She crossed her arms in a manner that exposed her noticeably large, long-fingered hands.

Julie stood up to speak. She said nothing for a few seconds, and not a sound or movement was made by anyone else as she formulated what she was going to say. There was no questioning that she was a welcomed addition to the Michigan, albeit an unexpected one.

"I'm Julie Furniture, age nineteen. I'll be twenty in a few days. I am the rebellious daughter—at least that is what my parents tell their friends—of a stockbroker father and an opera-singing mother. My mom and dad were divorced when I was a young girl. They have since remarried, and I hope they will stay that way; and they are

The Tiger Cruise

currently living in Manhattan. I've been fascinated with submarines ever since seeing the movie *The Hunt for Red October* as an eight year old.

"I suppose you are all wondering why I am also here on the Michigan. Well, I met some sailors in Hawaii at a beach party a couple of weeks ago. My parents have a home there. I thought the sailors said they were aboard the Michigan; but I think they lied, because I haven't seen any of them so far among this crew. One of them told me that their sub was going to Seattle. Then the other night I met Ginger. She told me she was going to try to see her son on the Michigan from a fishing boat. 'Can I go with?' I asked. She agreed.

"I am a concert pianist and am scheduled to play a concerto at the Hollywood Bowl along with the Los Angeles Philharmonic in about ten days—on a Friday evening." The entire mess hall of people suddenly came alive. They turned and looked in disbelief at Julie. They had a hard time believing what she had just said. "As I speak, I can envision my parents contacting my agent with the news that I am in a secret place and that I may not be able to make my appearance. What makes matters worse, I need to be playing the piano every day."

Julie looked over at Chief Thornbloom and asked, "Do you happen to have a piano on the Michigan?" As he shook his head *no* she quickly added, "I didn't think so. I don't know what I am going to do. If anyone has any ideas, let me know." She stopped and sat down, signaling she had completed her introduction. Julie was having a field day with the visual attention she was receiving from most of the men—both young and old.

As she finished, she turned and glanced at David for about three seconds. It was the second time she had done this during the introduction session. David wondered why she looked at him. *Maybe it was just a random glance,* he thought, *but maybe not.*

"I believe all of the introductions are now complete," Chief Thornbloom said as he stood up. "I want to go over some safety and emergency procedures, as well as what the schedule will be for the next few days. We'll be assembling and posting the Tiger Crew work schedule a day in advance since we are not certain for how long we'll be submerged. We'll have the first one up shortly.

The Tiger Cruise

"The medical corpsman will be available to treat any injury or to give medical assistance to anyone requiring it. He is located in the pharmacy and first aid office just down the hall from the engine room on the second level. Please inform the medical corpsman of any prescription drugs you currently take and the reason for their use. Smoking is permitted only in auxiliary machinery room number one. Also, the captain and I will be here after lunch if any of you have any questions." With that the Tiger Crew meeting was dismissed.

The remainder of the morning was spent by the Michigan Tiger Crew members socializing among themselves in the Great Lakes Café. They had all filled out the job sheets given to them at the beginning of the orientation session. The sheets had already been processed, and by noon the list of assigned jobs aboard the Michigan was posted on the bulletin board in the corridor outside of the mess hall. Each member was assigned a sailor to train him in the work. At the bottom was the note: "If any assignment poses a problem for you in performing the duties, please let your trainer know as soon as possible." The entire crew was happy with the assigned work details and saw it as an additional part of the adventure they had embarked upon. The schedule was to start the following morning.

Ginger and Julie were assigned to help in the kitchen. Ginger loved the idea. Julie saw it as something she had always wanted to do but never had the chance. Her mother never cooked, and their meals were always prepared by a chef. *Maybe I can learn to cook,* she hoped.

After lunch, most of the Tiger Crew and many of the Michigan crew gathered in the mess hall and waited for the captain to arrive. They also did what all of them seemed to do best— drink coffee and eat cookies. Soon Captain Wagner and Chief Thornbloom walked in and took a seat near the door. One of the cooks on duty poured two cups of coffee, placed four freshly baked cookies on a plate, and carried them over to their table. Captain Thornbloom was the first to speak. "Does anyone have any questions? We'll try to answer them."

There was a noticeable silence for about ten seconds before Bill Wallace spoke up and said, "Captain, there are some rumors circulating about a foreign submarine that is following us. Some say it's a Russian sub, some say it's a French sub, and one rumor even says

The Tiger Cruise

it's a North Korean sub. Can you give us any information that will give us some comfort?"

The Captain turned and gave his senior chief a wearisome look, as if he were asking, "How did these rumors get started?" Both men knew an answer was needed, or else the Tiger Crew may begin to have doubts about the Michigan's leadership, on top of the fear and mystery of an already shaky Tiger Cruise start.

Captain Wagner stood up to speak. "Let me be very honest with you. This is what we know: We do know that there is a foreign sub within our proximity and closer to the United States than we want it to be. What we don't know is exactly what country it's from. We have a pretty good idea; but until we confirm this with positive data or have verbal verification directly from the country of origin, we're not at liberty to say. Don't worry, however, because we have several of our fast-attack subs not far away from where she's located. I have to leave it at that. And let me add, we will keep you up to date as we get information from our sources. Does that give you a satisfying answer?"

The crew answered with a collective head shake and a joint "Yes."

"Are there any other questions?" Chief Thornbloom asked.

Gustav Minter then asked, "Is it true that because of our emergency situation, we are not allowed to send or receive any satellite transmission messages?"

Again the two seasoned naval officials glanced at each other. The chief took this one. "This is true." That was all he said, adding to the uncertainty in the minds of the Tiger Crew.

"What about church services?" Virginia asked with some hesitancy, eager to change the subject of the questions. "Are there any Sunday services on board the sub?

"I'm glad you asked, Ginger," answered Captain Wagner. "There is no rigid structure to religious services on the Michigan. As with the other nuclear subs, it all depends on the personnel that we have at any one time. If we have a chaplain on board we will ask him to conduct a service on a Sunday or Saturday night. If he is a Protestant, he can hold a Protestant service. If he is Catholic, he will hold Catholic services. He may even provide the materials for

The Tiger Cruise

the Catholic mass or a Protestant service. On one cruise we had a sailor who had attended a Jesuit college and he conducted a Catholic service. We may even have a sailor conduct a service in whatever his faith is."

Virginia raised her hand to indicate that he wished to ask a follow-on question. "What do you currently have on the Michigan?"

"Let me answer that question," Chief Thornbloom replied. "The Sunday service is led by none other than the young sailor who fished you out of the water. Not many attend the service, but it is open to all who wish to attend. We do not have any other religious services at this time since we do not have anyone wishing to conduct them. There is a regular Bible study on Thursday evenings conducted by one of our officers."

Captain Wagner raised his hand slightly, indicting he wished to add something. "My experience has been that most sailors tend to be very religious and will demonstrate their religiosity in a number of ways." The Captain stopped and remained quiet for a brief moment.

After a few more questions on a variety of subjects, the meeting broke up. Another of the sub's chiefs entered the mess hall and whispered something into the captain's ear, then the two quickly left.

At 7:00 p.m. Chief Thornbloom was joined by Captain Wagner, and they gave the Tiger Crew a tour of the Michigan. The captain explained what was going to be done with the sub in a two-year re-fit program. They also were shown the torpedo room and given an explanation of how the torpedoes worked. There were eight of them weighing six thousand pounds each. In the control room each member was allowed to look through the periscope and to sit and steer the sub for a moment. Photos were taken by the sub's photographer of each member of the Tiger Crew looking through the periscope. The only area of the sub they were not allowed to visit was the engine room with its nuclear reactor and engine.

George Tedson asked Captain Wagner how much the Michigan weighed.

"Thirty-six million pounds," was the answer.

During the tour David caught Ginger's ear. He wanted to talk to her in private. "Ginger, can we meet for coffee after this tour? I have something to ask you. Can we meet in the mess hall?"

The Tiger Cruise

"Let's do that," she answered.

After the tour David and Ginger walked together to the Great Lakes Café. Ginger found a table and sat down while David procured two cups of coffee and a couple of fresh-from-the-oven cookies. "What do you wish to talk to me about, David?" Ginger asked.

"Ginger, I would like you to formally introduce me to Julie when it is convenient for you. Tell me, does she ever say anything about me?"

Ginger looked at David over the top of her cup of coffee and answered, "Do you want the truth, David?"

"Give it to me, Ginger," he answered.

"She thinks you're weird. A nice guy, but a little strange."

David smiled and replied, "Well, that's a start."

"She also thinks you have an interest in her," Ginger added.

"That puts me half way to first base, doesn't it? David asked.

"But," Ginger said, "keep in mind that she probably has her eyes on some other sailors also. After all, there are many sailors on the sub to pick from."

David thought for a moment. "I guess that makes it a challenge for me," he said in a positive tone.

At 8:00 p.m. the two women decided to visit by themselves over a cup of tea. They sat down in the corner of the room where three tables had been pushed together at lunch time. It wasn't long before some of the Tiger Crew and sailors decided to join them.

Instead of having their own conversation, the men fixed their attention on the women and listened to them talk—something the girls found rude and invasive. The word had spread rapidly that both of these women were single and most likely available. Soon the discussion drifted to the subject matter on everyone's mind—what danger the reported foreign submarine was posing to the Michigan. One of the sailors, Matt Denver, was noticeably quiet, which indicated he probably knew more information than anyone else involved in the discussion.

"I didn't even know that North Korea had a Navy," Frederick Quanto stated quietly.

George Tedson then added, "So, how big are the torpedoes they might have?"

More questions were asked and opinions given. The conversation which had started out at nearly a whisper by the two girls suddenly became loud, with several conversations going on at one time.

Finally, Matt Denver jumped in and said, "Hey, guys, let's not jump to conclusions. Let's let the people who have more information take care of the situation."

With that the gathered group was quiet and some of them left.

A half hour later David walked in, helped himself to a cup of coffee and a cookie, and found a table and chair on the opposite side of the mess hall. He sat positioned so that he could see Julie—which he knew might be quite offensive to her, but he didn't care. The two of them made eye contact a couple of times. *Maybe there's a spark,* he thought. *Given enough fuel, time, and interaction, it may develop into a bonfire,* was his next thought. Where would the flame come from? He just needed to be patient.

* * * * *

The control room personnel were busy following the whereabouts of the foreign submarine using all of the information-gathering techniques at their disposal. This included the latest satellite transmission, but it was twenty-four hours old. There was one strange thing about the repeated sonar transmissions of the foreign sub. It moved in close proximity to the Michigan and did not answer any of the attempts to communicate with her, which had the sonar people mystified.

* * * * *

At 9:30 p.m. an announcement came over the PA. "All Tiger Crew members are asked to report to the mess hall at 9:45." The crew came in from almost every part of the Michigan except the engine room, which was off limits and plainly marked as such.

Captain Wagner walked in and addressed the assembly. "Fellows and ladies, I promised you I would keep you informed of our prog-

The Tiger Cruise

ress. It has been determined that the sub we are looking for—or, rather, is looking for us—is possibly a new type of foreign sub that we don't yet have a sonar record of. And, let me add, we have sonar records of almost every sub in the world. We know how our sonar reacts to each of them. We have nothing on this particular sub. This one is apparently making its maiden voyage and is either lost or has lost communication with its government. That's all the information that I have for you at this time."

Julian Chesney spoke up and asked, "Is there any other theory that has been offered up by our intelligence analysts?"

"We don't have access to any satellite contact," answered Captain Wagner, "so we don't know. I will tell you this: Our sonar people believe this sub has no intention of doing us harm. They have not opened their torpedo doors at all, and we don't believe they intend to open them. What about you people? Do any of you have any ideas why we are all of a sudden encountering a strange submarine within a short distance of a major submarine base?"

It was quiet for about ten seconds, and the captain got ready to leave the room. The subject matter under discussion was beginning to become uncomfortable for the captain and for most of the Tiger Crew. Suddenly, someone cleared his throat in back of the room as though he wished to add to the discussion. Most of the crew turned their heads in the direction where the sound came from. It was David Cordell. He had come in unnoticed through the side doorway. Julie was sitting close to where the captain was standing. She also turned around to look. "Do you have an idea or a theory, David?" the captain asked.

David paused momentarily then said, "Well, Captain, ever since I first saw the movie *The Hunt For Red October*, I have been fascinated by the story—especially with the crew of that sub. I sometimes wake up at night asking myself, 'Why did all of those Soviet officers want to risk death to escape to America?' And then I hear lately on the news how bad conditions are in other countries. Putting these two thoughts together makes perfect logic. Maybe a small crew of young officers and sailors from the navy of a politically or religiously oppressed country decided to risk their lives and deliver a newly created vessel to our government. Maybe they see no future for themselves where they are. Maybe they just want to be free."

It was suddenly quiet as all in the room contemplated what had just been theorized. At that, the captain dismissed the meeting and left with a captivated look on his face.

The day had been a busy one. Shortly after 11:00 p.m., David lay on his bunk with a small reading light trying to read a novel. He was unable to sleep. His mind was on two subjects: the mystery foreign submarine and the young pianist on the Michigan whom he had yet to formally meet. Now that he knew about her piano-playing ability, there was something that stirred his romantic spirit more than ever. He knew very little about her, so maybe it was just the association both of them had with classical music that attracted him to her. But everything about this young woman told him he should not get involved. He finally tried listening to some music on his headphones, and eventually he fell asleep.

Chapter 4

The Tiger Cruise—Day 3—Friday

All but a few of the Tiger Crew were at breakfast at 6:30 a.m. It was ham-and-eggs day, and the Tigers had worked up an appetite from the night before playing cards, attending meetings, engaging in intense conversations, and watching videos. The Great Lakes Café was set up so that a few sailors could watch videos while others could engage themselves in other activities. One of the walls had a large bookcase stocked with an assortment of DVDs and videos. Every submarine movie ever made was in the bookcase.

Some of the Tiger Crew members had come from the East Coast, so their internal clocks functioned on an earlier schedule. Gustav Minter from Hawaii was three hours behind the West Coast's schedule, and some of the men just weren't accustomed to getting up so early in the morning. All of them, although not openly discussing it, were quietly worried about the situation they were currently involved in—namely, the mystery of the foreign submarine and not knowing when they would be off the Michigan. Most of them had obligations at home, and they were not permitted to contact their families and explain their absence. Some of them were even jokingly talking about having to travel around the world before the crisis was resolved.

The Tiger Crew members sat at various tables—some with family members, some with the Michigan crew members, and some with members of the command. Some of the table talk this particular

The Tiger Cruise

morning was about the sub's two female crew members. The attitude toward the girls was not one of regret, but rather of delight, since the cruise was now more exciting.

Ginger thought it would be helpful if she took the initiative to formally introduce David Cordell to Julie Furniture. Their first encounter at lunch on Wednesday had not been the best. It was quite obvious to Ginger that Julie seemed to disliked David for some reason. She thought she knew what it was, but she wanted to see if she was right. First, Ginger needed to find out more about David, her lifesaver from the waters of the Strait of Juan de Fuca.

As she entered the Great Lakes Café, Ginger saw David sitting alone at a table in the corner near the video library. He was listening to some music on headphones and writing on a tablet. She quickly grabbed her food and found an empty table. Then she walked over to where he was sitting and said, "David, could you sit at my table, please?"

He took off his headphones, smiled at her and said, "Sure. Do you want to go swimming today?"

The question elicited immediate laughter from Ginger. "Not really!" she said still laughing. "But thanks again for saving my life. That was one day that I will never forget. I was frightened out of my mind and I'm still cold! Imagine ... being saved from drowning by the U.S. Navy!"

Ginger and David walked over to her table and sat down across from each other. Ginger knew that Julie was about to walk into the mess hall.

"Let me pray over our food," David said to Ginger. They folded their hands and David prayed quietly, then they began to eat. "Tell me about yourself, Ginger," inquired David. "You seem to be a very nice person."

"Like yourself? You're a believer, aren't you?" Ginger asked with a grin.

"How did you know?" David asked.

"Are you kidding? I see it in how you conduct yourself," Ginger answered. "Not everyone asks the Lord's blessing on his food in public. Only special people do that."

The Tiger Cruise

David looked at Ginger, his facial expression now serious. "I wasn't always like that, you know" he said. "There are a few of us sailors aboard the Michigan who pray over our food. Some of the other sailors try to avoid sitting with us for that reason. The rest don't care. Tell me, Ginger, why you are really here. Did you really just want to say hi to your son Jake?"

"Well, yes and no. I haven't seen Jacob for about a year, and I knew my ex-husband, Warren ... Jacob's dad ... would be among the Tiger Crew. Warren and I still communicate, mainly about family matters. We actually grew up in the same small town. Since our divorce four years ago, I have gotten my life together. I can see now that our broken marriage was as much my doing as Warren's. I had planned to meet Jacob when the Michigan docked in a few days at Bangor ... to let him know that I still love his dad. Beings I was in the vicinity and I knew Jacob would be surfacing out from the John Wayne Marina, I hired Freddie to take me fishing. Little did I realize that it would cause a big problem for the Navy. Now that I'm here, maybe we can talk and get a few things settled. I didn't think Julie and I would cause a U.S. Trident Nuclear Submarine to be submerged for security reasons."

"Well, I'm glad you're here. Maybe I can be another son to you for the next few days," David commented. "At least we can communicate on the same wavelength, if you know what I mean."

"Yes, I do know what you mean," she responded. "And you can certainly be my son for a few days. There are not many women who can claim they were saved from drowning in the ocean while getting onto a nuclear submarine."

Just then Julie walked into the mess hall. David immediately saw her and his eyes were glued to her. Ginger ceased her conversation, noticing that David was now interested in a different matter. She looked at him, then turned her head and looked at Julie.

"I suppose you wish you could have saved her the other day," Ginger suggested with a smile on her face.

David didn't answer Ginger for a moment, then brought his eyes back to her. "Not really. She may have asked for someone else to jump in to get her."

"I'm sure if it had been Julie, every sailor on the sub would have jumped in," Ginger speculated. "The older sailors and chiefs nearby probably never moved a finger to save me. But you'll notice that these same old guys have their eyes on Julie right now. They are not interested in middle-aged women. They are sailors, without a doubt."

Ginger motioned for Julie to come over to where they were sitting. At first Julie hesitated; but then seeing no other table had an empty spot for her, she slowly walked toward their table. As she approached them, it was apparent that Julie's interest in David was less than cordial. Both Ginger and David asked themselves the same question: "Why?" David assumed it was because they had little in common with each other. He was attracted to Julie, and she was a challenge to him. Her unpleasant feeling toward him made it even more challenging. A host of other sailors aboard the Michigan were also interested in this beauty, even some of the chiefs and officers—both married and single.

Julie was wearing some navy clothes Chief Thornbloom had issued to her. They seemed a little baggy, which, along with her Navy cap, made her look that much more attractive. The chiefs had started to discuss among themselves exactly how they were going to handle this particularly unusual and sensitive situation on their submarine. Julie was the main topic of discussion in the sleeping quarters by the silos, in the bathrooms, in the mess hall, and even in the control room. Her appearance, no matter what she wore, was better than any of the pinup photos on the walls of the bookshelf-type sleeping bunks. Someone had taken photos of her the day of her arrival, made copies, and distributed them to the other sailors—for a good price, of course.

Julie somewhat reluctantly sat down next to Ginger and started to eat a bowl of mixed fruit and drink some coffee. She looked only at the table and her food, avoiding David altogether. Ginger was ready to make the introduction.

"Julie, I want to formally introduce you to David. This is David Cordell. And, David, this is Julie Furniture. You have seen each other but have not been formally introduced."

"Hi, Julie," David said as he looked at her and smiled.

"Hi," Julie unenthusiastically responded.

The Tiger Cruise

David had rehearsed what he would like to ask Julie when the time was right and if he had the guts. *Julie, maybe you and I could sit together sometime at dinner or lunch, and you could tell me about your piano playing,* was his rehearsed question to her.

"Ain't gonna happen" would be her answer, he suspected. David guessed that half of the Michigan crew had the same general question stored in their minds. This trip may be the first time a young, beautiful woman had been on the Michigan, other than during special visits of girlfriends and family members on visitor's day when the sub was at the dock at the Bangor Naval Base.

"Julie, how long have you been playing piano?" David finally inquired.

She just sat there, not responding at all to David's question. *Maybe she didn't hear the question,* he thought. It was quite noisy in the mess hall.

Julie stood up and turned to walk toward the condiments table. "I need to get some cream for my coffee," she said softly.

As Julie walked away, David quickly wrote a note on his pocket tablet, showed it to Ginger, and then scratched over it.

As Julie walked across the room, the sailors suddenly became much quieter—again, their heads following her as she walked. She returned to the table in less than a minute carrying a small container of cream. She sat down, opened the cream container, and poured it into the cup of coffee in front of her. The sailors then resumed their eating and talking.

As Ginger set down her coffee cup on the table she asked, "Julie, what piano concerto are you going to play in a few days at the Hollywood Bowl?" It was the question on David's mind and on his tablet. Julie suddenly became animated, not realizing that David had put Ginger up to asking the question.

"I'm scheduled to play the Rack 2—Sergei Rachmaninoff's Second Piano Concerto," was Julie's answer. "However, right now it appears that won't be happening. They'll probably get a replacement artist. I'm ready for the concerto with the exception of two of the more difficult passages. I also need to keep my arms and hands in shape."

The Tiger Cruise

David wanted to ask Julie a question that would probably infuriate her. He hesitated but then blurted out, "Those two passages wouldn't be in the third movement, would they?" He was ready to duck in the event she would suddenly throw a cup of coffee at him. Instead, Julie took a sip of her coffee and spoke directly to David for the first time.

"How did you know that?" she asked with a surprised look.

David seized the opportunity and looked deep into her eyes as he answered, "I have the Rack 2 on a record at home and on a CD—both with the same orchestra and artist. My grandfather willed the record to me when he died, along with his entire record and CD collection. I have listened to it many, many times ... maybe over a hundred. There are many difficult passages, especially in the third movement."

"Who is the pianist and orchestra on that recording?" Julie asked.

David had hit on a topic that they were mutually interested in. Maybe he could keep asking her questions that would continue the discussion. "Vladimir Horowitz with Ormandy and the Philadelphia Orchestra."

Julie made no comment to his answer or his apparent knowledge of classical music. She suddenly got up and collected her tableware. Before walking away, she stopped and looked back at David. "I have no piano to practice those two passages," she said with obvious frustration. "Also, I really need to see the music, but I may have to do without. If we don't get off this sub, I may not need either of them." Julie turned and walked out of the room. David continued to look at her until she was completely out of the Great Lakes Café.

Ginger then turned to David and said, "I do believe you two have finally connected in an amiable manner. That's good, but I still wonder why she has, up to this point, treated you like dirt. I see no reason why she should. She's seems to be a nice girl."

"I think I know why," David answered, "but, then again, maybe I just look like a cruel person from her past. I'm no psychiatrist, but it seems to me she has some kind of war going on inside of her."

"I believe you are correct, David," Ginger responded.

David had great respect for Ginger and appreciated her insight and willingness to help him. He was starting to look to Ginger as the

The Tiger Cruise

mother he had lacked in his life. Ginger had a similar feeling. She could use another son.

"David, tell me about your parents," Ginger said, changing the subject.

He took a deep breath. "My mom is dead and I don't know where my dad is," he confided to Ginger.

"I'm sorry," Ginger responded, "What happened, David?"

He seemed reluctant to answer Ginger, but responded anyway. "It's a familiar story ... Dad leaves Mom, Mom takes up drinking, and then Mom finally becomes so depressed that she commits suicide."

"I'm sorry," Ginger said sympathetically.

David shrugged his shoulders and continued his life story. "My father has gone into hiding someplace ... probably to escape paying the back child support he owes the county where my home is. My grandparents raised me since I was in the third grade. They sent me to Bible camp, vacation Bible school, and made sure I was in Sunday school every Sunday. I do feel bad. Even cheated. But I have learned to deal with the situation involving my dad. Maybe God has a special purpose by allowing this to happen to me. Destiny is not always bad—it's what we do with it that builds character. So does the navy, of course."

"It appears you are attracted to Julie, aren't you?" Ginger asked.

"Yes," David answered, "and that's unusual for me, since I don't come in contact with many girls in the navy."

"Why is that?" Ginger asked with a puzzled look.

David moved closer to Ginger and whispered, "You see, when we stop at different ports—like Guam, Honolulu, Los Angeles, and Singapore—I don't go to the places the other sailors frequent. In fact, many times the captain and the chiefs ask me to try and keep the boys from getting into trouble. I have had to go into bars and break up fights and get them back to the sub. It's made me a little unpopular with some of the guys ... that is until the next day when they have sobered up. Many times they thank me."

Ginger's next question was to be expected. "Have you ever pulled my son out of a bar?"

David took a deep breath, closed his eyes, and answered, "I think I would rather not answer that question."

The Tiger Cruise

Ginger smiled as if she expected that answer.

For David, seeing Julie was "love at first sight." That was the good news. The bad news was that it may not be God's will for him to have a serious relationship with her. David wasn't sure what Julie's spiritual condition was, and that was very important to him. Based on his initial encounter with her on the first day of the cruise, he was quite sure they were not on the same wavelength spiritually. There was also the question of whether Julie would even consider going out with him. In the current situation, there was no dating on the sub—mainly because no females were allowed. But a cup of coffee or dinner together may be possible. He knew that many of the other sailors were thinking about asking Julie out also. David's love for classical music was probably the only thing he and Julie had in common. He was hoping this mutual interest would be the spark that would give him a better chance than the other sailors. But David also knew that if the Michigan were to surface tomorrow, he would never see Julie again.

* * * * *

Since there was no communications with the outside world, no one on the Michigan was fully aware of what most of the news media was reporting concerning the missing submarine. What was being reported was sketchy—where the sub was last seen, that there were two females who had been rescued and were onboard the Michigan, that there was a small fishing boat blown up, and that a two-billion-dollar strategic naval vessel and its crew, with its twenty-four nukes onboard, was in danger. To make matters worse, word was being spread that a newly designed North Korean fast-attack submarine was after the Michigan. The news media were having a field day.

* * * * *

It was late at night and at a corner table in the mess hall, Max Schroeder, Dave Simmons, and Brian Denver were comparing the plights of their marriage breakups.

The Tiger Cruise

"Tell me, Brian, what was the straw that broke the camel's back in your marriage?" Max inquired.

Brian quickly responded, "In my case it was more like the big boulder that broke the camel's back. It was when I came home early from a business trip and caught my wife in bed with the tree-trimming man."

"You're kidding!" was the reaction from Max and Dave in unison.

"That really happened?" Dave asked. "I thought a tree-trimming service only worked on trees."

"Who paid for the tree trimming, your wife or you?" Max asked. "Or, was it a negotiated deal?"

"I have no idea," Brian continued, "and I didn't really care at that point. They both quickly exited the house; and that's when I packed up my stuff, loaded the car, and left. I let her tell the kids when they came home from school and asked about daddy being gone. This happened only six months ago, and the lawyers are still fighting. Now I wonder about the meter man, the garbage man, and even the mailman." After a brief pause he said, "What about you, Max? What's your story?"

"Well, I think my story is one better than yours. My wife was and still is a genuine battleaxe. We fought from the minute we left the church after saying our 'I dos.' I don't know what I was thinking of when I married her. It was like five years in hell being married to her. The final straw came when she humiliated me in front of a PTA meeting one night and I walked out. Ah, but my story has a happy ending. Her lawyer, who is also from hell, fell in love with my wife when she hired him to represent her in our divorce. They have been married for two years now, and all I can say is that they both deserve each other."

It was the third member of the trio's turn to tell his tale. Dave Simmons was a very successful neurosurgeon and a very busy man. He looked at his two buddies and related his story. "Guys, I was married to a nurse I met when I was in college. She is probably the ideal wife, as I now realize. We married and I started my practice, but I also continued my roving-eye practice. One thing led to another ... many conquests. Then I made a big error. I bought a diamond necklace for a woman I had met. Her husband died after I did his brain surgery, and I asked her out a couple times. My error was that I mistakenly put the charge for the necklace on my wife's credit card, which I carried in my wallet. When my wife didn't receive the necklace for Christmas, she asked me about the charge. I think she was about to forgive me for that particular transgression, then one afternoon she followed me as I supposedly left to go to a conference in another city. I met another woman at a café and then we went to a motel. My wife followed and waited in the car until after one in the morning.

"She convinced the night clerk to give her a spare key, telling him she'd left hers in the room. She quietly entered the motel room where the woman and I were asleep in the bed. My wife grabbed the woman, along with her clothes, and threw her out of the room. The poor woman was stark naked. I slept right through the commotion. My wife than crawled into the bed and we both slept until morning. Later, she found out I was involved with other women and that was it. Marriage done."

"So what happened when you woke up in the morning?" asked Brian.

"I just told her we'd better get a divorce. I think she wanted to fight to save the marriage, but I didn't."

Their table grew suddenly quiet. The stories were all the divorced trio could take for one day. They continued to fill their cups and drink the Michigan coffee.

Chapter 5

The Tiger Cruise—Day 4—Saturday

William Wallace, the only black member of the Tiger Crew, was sitting alone in the mess hall at 4:30 a.m. There was a three-hour difference in time from his home in Kentucky. As a farmer he was used to getting up early every morning to do the chores, but he was having trouble sleeping on the Michigan. He was drinking his second cup of freshly brewed Michigan submarine hazelnut vanilla coffee when two other dads walked in. Chuck Madsen, the stockbroker, and Elmer Garrick, the carpenter, were also used to waking up early. They poured their coffee and each placed a hot, fresh pineapple sweet roll on a Michigan plate before sitting down at the same table where Bill was relaxing.

"Hey, Elmer," Chuck asked, "how can I fix my house without spending a ton of money?"

"What is the problem? What do you want to do to it?" Elmer inquired.

"Well, my basement wall has a crack where the blocks are cemented together," Chuck answered. "It's a horizontal crack about four feet long."

"It sounds like the ground is pushing on the wall from the outside of the house," Elmer commented. "Do any of your neighbors have a similar problem?"

"As a matter of fact, yes, they do," answered Chuck. "The lady across the street spent thousands of dollars about five years ago fixing it."

"I would ask a cement contractor to come over and give you a bid on fixing it," Elmer suggested. "Ask a bunch of questions and learn as much as possible about the problem, the causes, and the fix. Pick his brain. Then see if you can fix it yourself. Maybe you can do part of the work yourself and contract the remainder out. You may have to dig a trench on the outside of the house and push the wall out from the inside. It could be costly." Just then one of the sailors brought over the fresh coffee and topped off everyone's cup.

"I have a question for you, Chuck—you being a successful stockbroker," Bill said.

"Shoot, Bill," replied Chuck, "or maybe I shouldn't use that word on the sub."

Bill leaned over and whispered to Chuck, "I'm about to inherit $100,000 from a rich uncle who died last month. How should I invest it?" Bill asked. "Uncle Herman has become ground temperature."

"Throw a huge party for the Tiger Crew when we return to shore," Elmer broke in with a hearty laugh.

"Good advice, Elmer," Chuck replied. "I would first hire a financial advisor and get his advice. He'll have you list your current financial investments, your goals, and assets. He has a good grasp of the ever-changing laws that affect people our age and our financial and retirement concerns. I would make certain I had a good long-term health care policy, also. He'll probably advise you to put some or most of your money in a variety of IRA investments. Make sure you review your financial picture at least twice a year. If you have any left over, send some to me."

"Make sure you leave me your address when you get off the sub," Elmer broke in once again.

The three members of the Tiger Crew sat quietly and enjoyed the peaceful moment in the mess hall before the breakfast rush.

All of the Tiger Crew were on time for breakfast, except for Alex Perkins. He had been on his way to the mess hall, but his disorder had him polishing all the chrome and brass-plated fixtures on his way to the mess hall. He was wiping everything in his sight. The

The Tiger Cruise

Michigan had never looked shinier. His son Duane walked in and looked for his dad. Noticing he was missing, the young sailor went looking for him.

Captain Wagner walked unexpectedly into the mess hall and meandered around the tables to where Ginger and Julie were seated. He placed a folded-closed corrugated box he was carrying in front of Julie.

"What's this?" she asked with surprise.

Acting just as surprised, the captain responded, "I don't really know. It was sitting outside my room as I left just now. I nearly tripped over it. It has your name on it written with a felt marker. The ink from the marker is still fresh ... you can still smell it. I don't recognize the writing."

Julie gave a puzzled look to the captain, to Ginger, and to a few of the sailors at the next table. She wondered about the contents of the box and who the culprit may be who sent it.

The Great Lakes Café was crowded this morning. It was waffle day, and the cooks usually couldn't make them fast enough. The Michigan could stay under water for months if it had to—except for running out of food. Every few weeks it needed to surface to take on food and various other essential supplies.

Julie set aside her empty breakfast plate and slowly began to open the flaps of the corrugated box, taking out the contents one item at a time.

"What is that?" Ginger asked, then she answered her own question. "Oh, it's a roll of heavy felt."

Julie slowly unrolled the material and turned it over. Everyone close by was observing—not so much what was in the box but Julie herself. The sailors were captivated by the mere appearance of her and her every move.

"It's a felt keyboard!" Julie exclaimed excitedly. "I wonder if it's to scale. Does anyone have a tape measure?" she asked. Within two seconds five sailors had their tape measures in their hands with their arms extended toward Julie. She selected one and placed the piece of felt on two tables that had been pulled together. "Someone hold each end of the felt while I measure it."

The Tiger Cruise

Everyone was quiet as she stretched out the tape with her long arms. "Forty-eight inches ... exactly right!" she exclaimed. "Now let me count the keys." She carefully counted the keys while everyone looked on. "Exactly eighty-eight keys—fifty-two white and thirty-six black. This is how I'm going to practice the Rack 2! What else is in the box?" She next took out a CD player and a set of headphones. She looked around the room, puzzled by what seemed like more than a coincidence. *I wonder who did this,* she thought to herself.

"Maybe the Navy knew you were going to be on the sub and they sent it to you," Captain Wagner replied in a laughing tone of voice.

"I doubt that," a sailor from the back blurted out in a cynical tone of voice. "Not the Navy." The sailor ducked down as the captain looked to see where the comment came from. Julie placed the headphones over her ears, plugged in the cord, and pressed the play button on the CD player. She began to finger the notes. Within moments a big smile came over her face.

"It's the Rack 2!" she said loudly with great feeling, not realizing the volume her voice produced while wearing the headphones. "I can't believe this is happening!" she said as her voice broke and her eyes begin to mist.

Some of the sailors had difficulty wondering how a rebellious nineteen-year-old beauty could get so emotional while fingering a fake piano. Maybe she was no longer a defiant child and was now a disciplined person, some thought. Many of the sailors were in the same rebellious situation when they entered the navy and had not as yet changed. Some of them were in the process of letting go of their defiant nature. The navy was quickly changing them, some faster than others.

Julie listened for a short time and then lifted the headphones carefully off of her head. The sailors in the mess hall watching her were sitting still. The music from the headphones had been loud enough for most at the adjacent tables to hear as Julie fingered her felt piano.

"What else do you have in the box? Ginger asked.

"I don't know. Let's look," Julie answered. She took out a large envelope and opened it slowly. "It's the piano score for the Rack

2—the Rachmaninoff Piano Concerto Number 2. How did this all happen? This is too much of a coincidence."

Julie took the piano score, opened to a page in the last movement, and began to finger the notes. Then she placed the headphones on her ears and keyed the CD player to the last movement. It wasn't like having a real piano on the sub, but it was the next best thing. It would at least keep her mind on the music, help her to memorize the difficult passages, and—most importantly of all—keep her fingers, arms, and hands in shape.

Now she just needed to get off of the Michigan.

Jake Johnson, the sailor son of Ginger and ex-naval Chief Warren Johnson, sat in the mess hall thinking about the relationship between his mom and dad. It had been stormy ever since the year Jake graduated from high school. That was the same year his mom made the decision to become a Christian. Warren could not believe Ginger's changed life. She no longer had the desire to do many of the things Warren did, and they suddenly found themselves with very different lifestyles.

Now their son Jake was at a crossroads in his own life and was ready for change. He had met a new interest in his life. Ginger and Jake had changed churches soon after his mom's conversion, and the result was that Warren no longer attended any church. Ginger now recognized that this was a mistake—she should have continued to attend the same church with Warren. They continued to be friends after the divorce mainly for the benefit of their son.

Jake decided to write a note to his mom and dad to encourage them to consider reconciliation. He took his note pad and began writing. It took him two hours. The letter ended with a summary paragraph:

> *So, Mom and Dad, there is nothing that would make me happier than to see you two come together once again. I know you can work things out, and for the first time the navy will not interfere with your living together. Dad, you can spend your retirement growing roses for mom. You can have many years together. There is one other reason for my request—I*

now have a girl on shore that I would like to marry, and I want you to be a model for us to live by. An added bonus, we may even give you some grandchildren someday. Please consider reconciling.

Love, Jake

He made two copies, one for his mom and one for his dad, and placed the notes in his pocket. At the proper time, he would give the notes to them.

* * * * *

The identity of the foreign submarine was finally communicated to the Michigan via a very short satellite message. It was a North Korean fast-attack sub. No contact had been attempted by the Michigan with the enemy sub, other than the sonar transmissions, but it was no doubt aware that the U.S. Navy knew of its location. It was assumed the diplomatic corps was in contact with the Korean government—specifically their Navy. Maybe the North Korean sub was in some sort of mechanical trouble. Maybe it was a spy submarine. Or maybe it was a decoy. At any rate, the Michigan was under strict emergency measures. The sub was either not moving at all or moving very slowly due to undersea currents. No communications were emanating from the North Korean sub to anywhere. The fast-attack sub USS Indianapolis had its torpedoes programmed to hit and blow it up if needed. Other naval vessels were nearby, ready to fire torpedoes if necessary. It had the U.S. Navy and the North Korean Navy at a standstill.

The one theory in the mind of Commander Wagner, although a bizarre one, was the one David had briefly suggested in the Tiger Crew question-and-answer session—that the sailors on the North Korean sub were trying to escape their government. Maybe that crew indeed had decided to seek asylum in the United States. It seemed a bit unusual that a foreign sub would come this close to the U.S. if its officers were not defying its own government. But maybe the North Korean government was not telling the whole story. The commander of the Michigan decided to wait for further information and instructions before coming to any conclusion. Virtually all of the officers and crew aboard the Michigan had seen *Red October* several times and were aware of what happened.

* * * * *

Six of the dads were in the mess hall for their afternoon coffee and were discussing the foreign sub. Julian Chesney voiced his concern in a joking manner. "Boy, I wanted a little excitement on this cruise ... but not this much or this type. I wish the captain would give us an update or let us ask more questions."

"How many torpedoes does the Michigan have, and can the Michigan maneuver as well as the North Korean sub?" asked Frederick Quanto.

The rest of the kaffeeklatsch did not answer. They only shook their heads with their concern.

Ten of the more portly dads wanted to form a weight loss club. They based the need to take this action on the energy required to maneuver themselves down the main hatch when they first got on the sub and the task of climbing the many stairs. They also had experienced how well the navy was feeding the Tiger Crew as well as the regular crew of the Michigan. They all could envision what their waistlines would look like in a few more days if they did not curb their lifelong eating habits. Most of them agreed that the food on the Michigan was even better than some of the cruise ships they had been on in the past to the Caribbean and along the Alaskan Inner Passage. The name of the diet group was "The Fat Tiger Crew Dads." They also thought it would be helpful to do some exercising.

Julie and Ginger agreed to form an aerobics class that would meet for thirty minutes every day. Surprisingly, Captain Wagner had agreed as long as they conducted it on the top floor where the exercise area was located. There were two additional requirements: First, the girls would have to wear full-length sweat pants that the navy would provide. Second, one of the sailors would assist them to keep it official. When it was announced that Julie and Ginger would lead

The Tiger Cruise

the class, there were twenty sailors that volunteered for the class in addition to the tiger dads.

Captain Wagner had some concerns about this activity. He wasn't so worried about the safety of Ginger. It was Julie that concerned him. She had most of the young sailors—single and married—awestruck. These sailors had been at sea for months with only short breaks while stopping for the sub to take on food and supplies. There was no telling what might take place with twenty sailors watching a twenty-year-old beauty do her exercises. However, since there was not an end time in sight for the cruise, he concluded the undertaking probably would be beneficial and healthful. Furthermore, COB Stengel and many of the officers and chiefs agreed and approved.

It was about noon when word was received that Tiger Crew member Alex Perkins had fallen and hit his head on a railing. He was treated for a suspected concussion and sent to his bunk for rest. Apparently, he was in one of his OCD routines, polishing some chrome, when he tripped backwards and hit his head. He was out cold for forty-five minutes before an emergency crew brought him back to consciousness. They carried him to the examining bed in the sub's pharmacy, then to his bunk where a couple of the dads were assigned to watch him. They would take turns, along with Alex's son Duane. Since there was no x-ray machine on board, and since the sub could not surface for medical treatment, the only option was to keep him under observation.

It was barbequed ribs night on the Michigan. It was also the night when many of the sailors came to the mess hall with a pair of latex gloves in order to eat the ribs without getting their hands and clothes messed up. It was the only way to eat these ribs. If the chiefs would allow it, many of them would come to the mess hall with only a pair of shorts on, and maybe a bib around their necks. The ribs were smoked, frozen, then drenched with the best barbeque sauces that the Navy could find. Roasted vegetables with an herb sauce were served alongside the meat. It was also make-your-own-banana-split night.

At 8:00 p.m., a panel discussion was planned for the Tiger Crew. Captain Wagner and three of his chiefs were scheduled to tell the crew the purpose of the Trident subs and, specifically, the Michigan. All of the crew was gathered. Ginger and Julie sat together at one corner of the group. They all sat around one large table made by shoving together six tables, with the panel members at one end.

David was still in the kitchen at the end of his shift at 8:00 when the meeting started. The panel discussion was late getting started and David, although not invited, decided to join the group. He found an empty chair away from the group and sat down just as the session began. He was enjoying a dessert, cherry cream cheese pie, along with some coffee.

Each member of the panel gave a brief description of their particular role in the functioning of the sub and some of the typical problems encountered on their trip around the Pacific Rim. Questions were asked and answered, and the session was over by 9:00. The members of the panel departed for their quarters, and the Tiger Crew then gathered for card playing and socializing.

David saw an opportunity, so he picked up his coffee cup and moved over to an empty chair next to Julie. If he hadn't moved when he did, some other sailor would have done the same. Ginger was sitting on the other side of Julie. Since it was his move, he decided to speak first. "How are you girls doing?" he asked.

"We're fine," both of them answered, almost in unison. Ginger and Julie had become good friends.

"How are *you* doing David?" Ginger asked. "We haven't seen much of you in the last day or so."

"I'm ready for a leave," David responded. He was hoping Julie would ask the next question so he could talk to her directly. She did.

"What are you going to do on your next leave?" she asked.

David was surprised that she spoke to him, but he liked the question she asked. "With our current circumstances, it depends on where we land," he answered, "and when we land. Normally, I will find a beach to swim at, maybe do some waterskiing, rent a car and do some sight-seeing, or take in a ball game. If it's Sunday, I will try to find a good church and attend services. I make sure I have my uniform on so someone will invite me to their home for din-din."

The Tiger Cruise

"That sounds like a sailor," Julie said.

Ginger all of a sudden stood up. "Excuse me, I need to leave for a bit," she said.

It was quite obvious to both Julie and David that Ginger's departure was intentional. David was now alone with Julie—or as alone as a couple could be on a nuclear submarine in the mess hall. He sat quietly until Julie spoke to him once again.

"David, let me ask you a personal question. Do you have a girl in every port, like all sailors?" It wasn't exactly the question he was expecting, but he was ready to make good use of the lead-in.

"What do you mean?" he asked.

"You know," she continued, "as a sailor, do you have much time or any chances to go out with girls in the ports where the Michigan stops? Do you have any romance in your life? Or is it all navy for you?"

This is going to be a difficult question to answer, he thought. But he would never have a more opportune moment than this one with this particular beautiful young lady. God would have to give him something to say. He looked directly at her and said, "Well, do you really want the truth, Julie?"

"Yes, I do," she answered.

"When we come into a port, I don't know any girls and I don't go to the bars and night clubs where the other sailors usually go to meet girls. So, consequently, I just don't meet girls—that is, until this trip." He stopped and continued to look at Julie.

"What do you mean 'until this trip'?" she asked.

David continued, "Until this trip, when I first saw you in the fishing boat and on top of the sub, girls were on my list of things only to think about. I had never seen a girl like you. And that is the truth." Julie just looked around the room. David felt ill at ease about what he had just said to her. But he was telling her the truth.

"Well," she said, "I never expected that answer. I'll need to think about that."

"I don't want to ruin this moment by saying anything further, like I sometimes do." he said. "Just let me conclude with this: The truthful answer to your question is there may be times in my life when I will meet other girls, and I am sure God has a nice girl picked out for me. I will meet her someday. I'll just have to wait."

"What does God have to do with it, anyway?" she inquired in a cynical tone.

David looked down and remained quiet. *I've said too much,* he thought. But he decided to continue the discussion by becoming philosophical. He looked at Julie and gave his answer to her question. "Usually discussions about the future involve words like destiny, serendipity, chance, fate, and so on. Most people think events in life such as meeting people are random happenings. I don't think so."

Julie got a puzzled look on her face and came back with additional questions. "So, what are they, then? And what or who causes events to happen? Is it some giant central processing unit or astrophysical or cosmic force? Don't we cause things to happen? What are you talking about, David?"

"How about if we include in the options you just mentioned a Superhuman Individual?" David answered.

"David, I don't know if you are a dazzling person or a little crazy. What are you suggesting?"

"How about a Supreme Being?" David asked forcefully.

"You mean God, don't you?" Julie whispered clearly.

"Bingo! You've got it, Julie!" David answered quietly, but forcefully.

Julie decided to challenge him in his seemingly wild theory. "Let's hear you prove this wild theory of yours ... that God causes things to happen and causes things not to happen and causes people to meet each other."

David had to think quickly. He knew what he believed, but could he explain it so that Julie would understand what he believed? "Let's try this, Julie. You are scheduled to perform the Rack 2 at the Hollywood Bowl in a few days. Correct?"

"Correct," Julie answered.

"Is the Rachmaninoff Second Piano Concerto a good composition?" David asked.

Julie was quick to answer, "It is probably the most popular and most romantic piano concerto ever composed. It takes great piano technique and power in the pianist's fingers, hands, and arms, along with a good orchestra. It has beautiful melodies and is orchestrated without any flaws. It's perfect."

David waited for a few seconds and then continued. "Now Julie, did Rachmaninoff just happen to find this piece of music along the road one day?" he asked a little condescendingly.

"Of course not," Julie answered in a defensive mode. "He spent many years studying, playing, composing, and performing many works before creating this great concerto. Furthermore, it was composed after going through great hardship and disappointment in his life."

"Do you think all of what you just said contributed to the success of the Rack 2?" David asked.

"Yes, I sure do." Julie answered.

"So there was a purpose for all of those hardships and disappointments in Rachmaninoff's life," David replied in a courteous manner, attempting to move toward a logical conclusion. "Now, do you think all of those contributing factors happened by chance to Sergei, or did God decide He wanted to bless Rachmaninoff, the music world, and you, with a work that sounded like it was made in heaven and that even His angels would rejoice in hearing it?"

Julie continued to look at David but said nothing.

David continued his reasoning, hoping to make a powerful point with his conclusion. "What about you and I meeting each other? Think of all of the things that have happened in and around the Michigan submarine in the past few days. Do you think just maybe God caused or allowed those things happen so that you would be placed on this sub, and that meeting you would be a blessing to me?"

Julie sat quietly in a contented manner. She had never thought about the seemingly random events in life in the manner David had just explained. Maybe she wasn't fully convinced, but she began thinking in a different direction — in the direction that David believed. She had never received such a beautiful complement from anyone like the one David had just given her.

David got up from his chair and looked at her, and added one final thought. "And just think, Julie, of how many thousands of other people you will bless at the Hollywood Bowl when you play the Rack 2." Enough said. David decided it would be best to let her think, and he quietly walked out of the mess hall.

Chapter 6

The Tiger Cruise—Day 5—Sunday

The fifth day of the cruise started with two sounds of terror to the Tiger Crew. The first, at exactly 2:00 a.m., was the sudden abrupt announcement on the sub's PA system, "DIVE! DIVE!" This was a routine daily occurrence, but it was the first time it had happened at this quiet hour when all of the Tiger Crew were asleep.

The second piece of excitement occurred a few seconds later during the actual dive. A shot rang out in one of the sleeping areas. There was a muffled scream from the middle bunk of the three-tiered set of beds just a few feet away from one of the nuclear silos.

The sleeping quarter was soon buzzing with navy medical personnel. One of the sailors had been shot while he was asleep. The sailor had for some reason decided to sleep differently. Ever since he had come on the Michigan some three months previously, he had slept with his feet where his head had been. For some reason the sailor had decided to change his sleeping position for the night, which probably saved his life.

All of the sailors and Tiger Crew members sleeping in the adjacent bunks heard the commotion and were quickly out of bed. Immediately, medical assistance was provided. Captain Wagner and COB Stengel were alerted and raced to the area where the shooting had taken place.

The medical team applied first aid to the wound. No bones were broken, but a bullet had lodged into the top of sailor's foot. The bullet would have to be removed as soon as possible.

The Tiger Cruise

The one Tiger Crew physician onboard had been sleeping in the next stack of beds and had awakened with all of the commotion. He was observing the medical team as they were evaluating and treating the sailor's injury. Dr. Dave Simmons stepped forward and volunteered to help. "I've removed many bullets before ... most of them from the brain. Let me have the honor of this one."

The captain thought for a moment and then said, "Let's get it done. It will save us an emergency trip to an onshore hospital, and we can't surface at this time anyway. Will you need anything other than what we have in our medical room?"

Dr. Dave quickly answered, "First, let's get him to the examining cot in the sub's pharmacy."

The sailor was carefully carried down the hall and up the stairs to the small room where most of the first aid on the Michigan was carried out. "What's your name, sailor?" asked Dave.

"Don Denert," the sailor replied.

Dave placed his hand compassionately on Don's shoulder and said, "I'm going to deaden your foot so I can remove the bullet. You shouldn't feel a thing. The bullet is not in very deep."

The COB stepped into the room and asked the sailor, "Do you remember hearing anything, like someone running away from the area?"

"Negative," answered the wounded sailor. "I was fast asleep when I heard the shot and felt a pain in my foot."

Within twenty minutes the bullet had been removed, and Don was back in his bunk resting.

By 4:00 a.m. the entire Tiger Crew had been alerted to the shooting and was being asked to go to the mess hall for a meeting with the sub's command. Julie and Ginger were also there.

Captain Wagner called for everyone's attention and said, "As you are most likely aware, we have just had a shooting in one of our silo bunk areas. We're not sure what exactly happened, but I have put one of my chiefs on the case full time until we find the person responsible. Until we find him, or her, or whatever happened, everyone onboard the Michigan is a suspect." The captain momentarily glanced at the two women.

The Tiger Cruise

"Everyone except the victim," Dave Simmons added.

"Not so," countered Captain Wagner. "The gunshot indeed may have been self-inflicted. We cannot rule out anyone or anything. We are cordoning off the area where the shooting occurred. Until further notice, stay away from that area and stay alert to anything that would give us a hint. We'll be talking to the regular Michigan crew within the next couple of hours. That's all for now." With that the captain departed. Everyone sat quiet and worried.

The breakfast atmosphere was unusually quiet. All of the Tiger Crew was worried that they might be the next victim of a madman aboard the Michigan. The two women decided to sit with the rest of the group for extra security. They also were very quiet.

After eating, Julie moved to a less crowded area in the mess hall and commenced practicing on the felt piano. This took her mind off of worrying about the shooting incident. If the room became crowded, she would roll up the piano and just listen to the CD player and follow the score. She needed to practice and concentrate for as many hours a day as possible.

David came in off of his night watch duties. He got his breakfast and walked to the closest table available. It was not particularly busy at 8:00 a.m., and the music from the headphones could be heard clearly. David recognized it as being the last movement of his favorite piano concerto—the Rack 2. Many of the younger and older sailors had their eyes fixed more on Julie than their ears on the music. She loved receiving the attention. David enjoyed the music as well as watching Julie.

At noon everyone on the Michigan was still nervous about what had happened ten hours earlier. The chief investigating the incident looked at everyone's file to see if there might be something that could indicate an unstable personality or a possible motive. This included both the sub crew and the Tiger Crew. Both the captain and COB couldn't believe someone would purposely shoot someone else on their sub. There had to be some other explanation.

Nothing like this had ever happened on the Michigan or any one of the other thirteen Trident Nuclear Subs. Witnesses in and

The Tiger Cruise

around where the shooting took place were interviewed without any credible leads. The shooting victim had no known enemies either on or off of the sub. Sailor Denert was a first-rate sailor according to his file and his chiefs. He had received several awards. What had happened was a complete mystery to everyone.

* * * * *

In the command center the work of keeping track of the mystery submarine continued. There were many similar submarine sonar patterns in the Michigan's library, but none matching this one. It was a fast-attack sub, however, and was armed with torpedoes. What was this foreign sub up to, the sonar personnel all wondered.

* * * * *

Shortly after lunch, Fernando Perez, the tall detective from San Antonio, Texas, decided to pay the commander a visit. He had an idea he could be of some assistance in the investigation. He walked through the command center and knocked on the door of the commander's quarters. Fernando was greeted with a loud "come in!"

Fernando stuck his head in the door and said, "Howdy, Captain. Could I bother you for a minute? I thought maybe you might let me lend a hand on your shooting investigation. With my experience, I may be able to shed some light on it."

The commander stopped what he was doing, suddenly very interested, and motioned for the Tiger Crew member to enter and sit on a three-legged stool. "Sure," the captain answered. "We need a break on this one. What do you know?"

"Well," answered Fernando, "as a detective back in San Antonio, I have investigated a whole host of shootings. Without meaning any disrespect to you or your fine crew, I may be able to find something your boys might have missed."

"We certainly are not equipped or prepared to investigate attempted-murder cases on this boat, and I would welcome any input you can give us. Where would you like to begin?" the captain asked.

"Let me go to the crime scene and have a look-see. There has to be some clues right there in the bunk area."

"You know, I was about to do that myself. Why don't we walk down there and take a peek." They left the captain's cabin, climbed down the steel ladder, and walked down the hallway to the sleeping quarters of the enlisted crew members.

Once Fernando and the captain entered the crime scene, they looked the area over for anything that would give them a clue. The detective had conducted similar investigations numerous times in his many years of crime scene work in San Antonio. "What does the bullet look like?" Fernando asked.

"I believe it's still in the sub's pharmacy," the captain answered. "Dr. Simmons put it in a plastic bag after he dug it out." Commander Wagner got on the phone and asked someone to bring the bag to the sleeping quarters.

Soon they were examining the lead bullet for any significant clues. Fernando was the first to offer a comment. "This bullet is used with an antique gun—at least this type of bullet is. I've seen it and the gun at flea markets and gun shows in Texas many times. The gun is worth a lot of money on the antique gun market. Do you have anyone aboard who may deal in antique guns?"

The commander stroked his chin with his left hand as he thought for a moment. "I can't think of anyone," he answered.

"I hate to even ask this question, but what about anyone from the Tiger Crew?" Fernando asked. "Do any of them have antique guns as a hobby?"

"Let's check the files and ask around," was the commander's response.

Fernando again looked closely at the bullet as he lifted it up to a bright light on the ceiling. "Wait a jerk. Let me look at something," he said. He walked over to the area on the opposite side of the silo bunk area where three other beds were located. The officer carefully examined the top bunk. After several seconds he said, "Well, looky here! See what we have?"

The captain walked over and looked where Fernando was pointing. "I see gunpowder burns and black marks," the captain responded. "Can that be from a bullet exploding?"

The Tiger Cruise

"Yes, it can," answered Fernando. "I think the bullet somehow exploded and hit the sailor in the foot. Also, there are no marks on the bullet from the barrel of a gun."

The captain did a little celebration dance and firmly shook hands with the Spanish-American officer. "Boy, am I glad you came along!" the captain responded. "This is one item off my worry list. Now I can work on the other troubles on my list."

An announcement on the PA system brought the Tiger Crew to the mess hall within five minutes. Captain Wagner, COB Stengel, and Officer Perez walked in and stood in front of them. Brian Denver was the first to speak. "What tidings of bad news do you have this time?"

"Actually, some good news," the COB answered. "We have solved the shooting of our sailor." Applause rang out for only a few seconds as the Tiger Crew were anxiously waiting for an explanation from one of the three people standing in front of them. "I will let Officer Fernando Perez tell you about it."

Fernando cleared his throat and said, "Tigers, it was an antique bullet that exploded when the Michigan performed its dive exercise early this morning. The antique bullet apparently had deteriorated to the point that it would take little to explode it. The salt in the air probably made it corrode faster than usual. As the Michigan made its dive, it produced a force that caused the bullet to fire. The bullet was lodged in one of the unattended bunks across from where Sailor Denert was sleeping. How it got there and how long it's been there is an unsolved mystery. Perhaps it was accidently left there by a sailor who previously occupied the bunk who may have been an antique gun collector. At any rate, the shooting has been solved."

There were some questions asked and answered prior to the breakup of the short meeting, but everyone was glad and relieved.

It was Sunday and the only religious observance of the day on the Michigan was to be a short thirty-minute service held in the mess hall at 3:00 p.m. David had volunteered early in the cruise to lead the services since there was no one on the Michigan with any seminary training. Normally, a Navy Chaplain was part of the Michigan's crew.

The service usually started with the singing of a familiar hymn or two. Then there was a short prayer by the leader, and anyone who wished to offer prayers or petitions was encouraged to participate. Next was the reading of a short passage of scripture by one of the sailors, followed by some comments by David. A short prayer and benediction concluded the service. Coffee and fellowship usually followed.

The service was usually held in the library since there were not many who attended and a large space was not needed. Today, however, the Tiger Crew was invited and a few more than normal were expected, so the mess hall was chosen for the service.

Ten of the Tiger Crew dads showed up for the service, along with Ginger and Julie. Julie was hesitant about attending, but Ginger talked her into it. Just before 3 p.m., many of the regular Michigan crew walked in, as did Captain Wagner and some of his officers and chiefs. The Great Lakes Café was suddenly a chapel! *What's the reason for the increase in attendance?* David wondered. Maybe it was because of the heightened security threat. Or maybe the two women onboard created an opportunity for the sailors to enjoy seeing what they had missed for the past months. Or maybe it was that they had nothing else to do.

David welcomed everyone to the service and led in two verses each of the hymns "The Old Rugged Cross" and "Amazing Grace." The Lord's Prayer was recited by the gathered group, then one of the sailors read a chapter from the Psalms. David then spoke on the theme, "What God Expects Us to Do." He told the Sunday service attendees, "God expects us to do what our duties are as assigned by those He places in command of us, and to do them to the best of our ability with honesty and with purpose. If you are placed in a difficult situation or location, just bloom where you are planted and don't complain. If you do all of this, you will be doing God's will."

David spoke for about ten minutes, then told the group, "I would like to pray for several things this afternoon. If any of you have specific prayer requests or concerns, please feel free to state them now." There was a short pause while this unexpected opportunity was contemplated by those present.

Finally, Brian Denver spoke up. "David, can you pray for my daughter who is about to have my first grandson? She is bedridden because of toxemia."

"What is her name?" David asked.

"Betty," he responded.

"Are there any other prayer requests?" David asked.

Again there was a short interlude of silence, then a young sailor spoke up. "I am afraid that when we return to base, I will be met by the lawyer my wife has retained. We have been having some problems, and the last thing she told me before I left was that she wants out! Maybe you could pray that she will wait and we can work things out. I want her to meet me at the dock when we return."

At that point no one was moving, and only the ventilation system was audible. All of the Michigan crew knew very well that this was a big worry for many of the sailors.

After a couple of more prayer requests voiced by a few of the worshipers, David prayed. He prayed for the requests and then ended with a few of his own requests. "Lord, protect the Michigan in our current difficult situation. Be with our chiefs and officers as they direct our activities and work. Be with Captain Wagner and give him great wisdom as he makes important decisions. Protect the families of all who are on this sub and give them comfort."

Julie had been sitting quietly all through the service with her eyes either closed or looking down. She didn't want to be there. She suddenly came alive with what David prayed next. "Lord, please cause the Michigan's current situation to be resolved in time for Julie to perform at the Hollywood Bowl. Keep her arms and hands strong even without a piano." That and a brief benediction ended the service.

Julie suddenly felt both an embarrassment and a sense of appreciation and comfort for the prayer David had prayed. During the coffee hour, she thanked him and said, "I am glad I came today."

It was pork chop night at the Michigan Great Lakes Café. They were large, thick, and breaded. The sailors were allowed as many as they wanted. Also on the menu were candied sweet potatoes, and caramelized rice. For those watching the scales, there was the ever-present and healthy salad bar. Many of the sailors, as well as the Tiger Crew, chose the healthier alternative. The Navy was serious about the Michigan crew needing to be in shape at all times.

Once the meal was finished and the mess hall had been cleaned, tables were arranged for the evening's recreation. Sunday was bingo night, and a few of the sailors had gathered to try their luck at winning. The prizes were not that great, but they did provide some incentive for the participants.

David walked into the mess hall. Seeing Julie sitting alone, he walked over to where she was and sat down. "I hope you don't mind if I sit here," he said.

"You may," she said.

"May I ask you a question?" David asked, attempting to start a conversation.

"Sure. Shoot." Julie answered. "Oops ... probably not the word to use today.

"Tell me about your parents," David said, still chuckling from her comment. "I know your dad is an investment broker and your mom sings opera."

Julie took a deep breath and looked at David, her big brown eyes stabbing directly into his heart. She answered, "There's not much to tell beyond that. They met when Dad was in the army in Germany. Mom was on tour singing Wagnerian opera, and Dad had some free tickets for the afternoon performance of *Die Meistersinger*. He had some good box seats on the side—almost directly above the stage—and could see mom clearly even without his binoculars. She noticed him looking at her. He was alone and thought he would attempt asking her for dinner after the opera. He went backstage, saw her standing with other singers, walked right up to her, and asked her out to dinner. Since they were both from New York City, she accepted. I think it was his uniform that attracted her to him.

"Unfortunately, the marriage has been a rocky one. I think the combination of my piano playing career and my rebelliousness has kept them together. They divorced once and got remarried, have separated a couple of times, and are now once again together. I don't know what's wrong with them. Maybe they will stay together this

The Tiger Cruise

time. They will be in Los Angeles to see me play, if I ever get off of this sub on time."

David was fascinated by her parents' story and by Julie's charm. An added bonus was that she may someday be an international pianist. He needed to keep priming the pump by asking her questions. "They must have loved you very much to provide you with the musical training you had. How old were you when you started playing the piano?"

"I was actually four years old when I took my first lesson in Manhattan. My first piano teacher lived across the hall in our apartment building for three years and provided free lessons. In exchange, my dad gave the lady free financial advice—like where she should put her money. He also did her income tax. My dad got the better deal, I think. To be honest with you, playing the piano is about the only area of my life where I displayed any discipline. Like I said, I have given my parents fits with my rebelliousness. Maybe that is what has kept pulling them back together. They even sent me to a Bible camp one summer when I was fourteen."

"How did that work out for you?" he asked. David had an idea how she was going to answer this question. He needed to be ready to respond—or maybe not respond at all.

"Terrible! I couldn't stand all of the garbage they were feeding me. Excuse me for saying that in front of you. The kids were nice and I learned all of the songs. I was asked to accompany the singing on the piano and they had me play a recital for the parents on the last day. But I just couldn't buy all that Bible stuff they were feeding us. Have you ever been to a Bible camp?"

David now had an opening to talk about himself and his life, but had to be careful how he approached it. He didn't want to upset Julie. "Yes, I have. Several times. My grandparents sent me to one in northern Minnesota."

"How did you like it?" Julie asked.

"I enjoyed it very much. That's where I made the greatest decision of my life—one of the 'big two' decisions a person can make in life."

"What was that important decision you made?" Julie asked in puzzlement.

"I decided that I would accept the Creator of the universe as my personal Savior," David answered in a very positive tone of voice.

Julie once again rolled her eyes. She had to say something back to David. "Well, maybe that's okay for you ... but not for me," she countered. "I think you're crazy ... and simpleminded."

David never expected her to say that, and it made him feel slightly humiliated. But that was to be expected, he figured. He didn't know how to respond without offending her. Julie also felt bad about what she had just said and she didn't know why she said it.

"Then you have made that decision already," David responded.

Julie sat and looked guilty. She understood what David meant. "I guess you and I aren't on the same wavelength," Julie commented. She turned her head and looked to the other side of the room, not responding further on that topic. Then she looked at David and asked with great interest, "What is the other important decision in life?"

This is a question that might be easier to answer, David thought, *but maybe not.* "It's the decision a person makes when he or she chooses the person to marry," David said. He decided to not go any further with the subject unless she asked. She did.

"What do you mean by that?"

"Maybe you could ask Ginger to explain it to you," he answered. "She has had firsthand experience. They say marriage can be a happy time, or it can be a hell on earth. Just ask our divorced Tiger Dads."

"Well," Julie concluded as she got up to leave, "you can keep all of your ideas on religion and God. It's not for me." With that she walked out of the room.

David sat stunned. He thought he might have a chance to break through to Julie's heart. There was a war going on inside her, and he now knew for sure what it was. She couldn't be happy or find fulfillment with her life and career until she was at peace with her Maker.

David went to his bunk and tried to fall asleep. He was disappointed, mad at himself, and somewhat confused. On the one hand, he needed to clear this young professional out of his mind, and he figured that was what God wanted him to do. On the other hand, he couldn't keep his mind from thinking about her. *Maybe tomorrow will provide another opportunity for me to interact with her in a more positive manner.* Or maybe it would get even worse.

Chapter 7

The Tiger Cruise—Day 6—Monday

The situation with the North Korean submarine that the Michigan was tracking was still very strange. There was very little noise emanating from it, their torpedo tubes were not open, and there was no transmission of messages from it to anywhere. It was sitting like a dead and floating sea creature. Another strange occurrence was puzzling to the Michigan command: the sub was following the Michigan wherever it went. Captain Wagner decided to go to the control room at 4:00 a.m. and ask his sonar operator what he thought. "What occurred overnight, Mike?"

Mike Mullinix was a fifteen-year veteran sailor who had been on three different boomers and two fast-attack subs. He was also an experienced sonar engineer. Mike was quick to answer, "We have been at six hundred feet for eight hours now—just sitting here. In that time our 'tagalong' has not moved an inch. I think some of the whales think that she's their mama. When we move one hundred feet one direction, she moves one hundred feet in that direction. If we move fifty feet up, she moves fifty feet up. If we move fifty feet back down ... well, you get the picture. It's as if they are trying to tell us something. We can detect only some very slow and quiet movement inside her. What should we do next, Captain?"

Captain Wagner looked at his expert sonar sailor and answered, "Let's move around a bit more and see what happens. Let me know

The Tiger Cruise

of anything unusual." Captain Wagner rose from his chair to leave. "In the morning, let's increase the speed. See if she follows us."

On the surface, the U.S. Navy was busy tracking the Michigan and the tagalong using satellites and tracking ships. The press and news services were having a field day going on rumors and so-called experts in their reporting of the lost sub. The North Korean Navy and government were completely silent on the subject. Satellite records showed that the sub left its base in North Korea and slowly moved into the Pacific Ocean, then all of a sudden increased full speed toward the northwest coast of the United States. It finally stopped a few hundred miles off the western coast.

* * * * *

Julie's parents were doing all they could to convince the people at the Hollywood Bowl to keep her on the concert program with the philharmonic symphony. As normal, an alternate artist had been found in case of her cancellation. Since she had been reported to be on the lost submarine, ticket sales for the concert had been brisk and the Bowl was close to being sold out. There were even reports of scalpers making a profit off of ticket sales. Because of the increased publicity, Mr. and Mrs. Furniture were convinced that a huge, successful concert at the Hollywood Bowl would rocket Julie into an international career.

The families of the Tiger Crew were very worried—filled with anxiety and fear as to how the crisis would finally turn out. The Navy kept them in the news loop with as much as they could. All the Navy could do was inform them that their family members were safe on the submarine and being protected by other navy vessels.

The Michigan medical officer was working with the Tiger Crew members who were on critical medications to make sure the doses in their possession were stretched out as far as possible.

* * * * *

The Tiger Cruise

At 6:00 a.m., it was time for the morning aerobics session. The sailor assigned to be Julie's assistant could not make it for the session. Since he did not have anything to do until his regular work shift at noon, Captain Wagner asked David to assist. Julie and Ginger were not informed of this change in plans, but they didn't seem to mind when he showed up.

Most of the sailors used the exercise equipment in the gym area on the top floor of the Michigan. They were required by the captain to keep in top shape while on the sub. Most of the sailors had a maximum weight requirement and needed to stay below that critical weight. Climbing the steps between the three levels on the Michigan was a big incentive to lose weight. The Tiger Crew had the same motivation to keep in shape.

Julie started the music on the boom box, and the ten Tiger Crew and sailor participants began to do the exercises as Julie directed. She was a very agile woman of almost twenty years, in excellent physical shape, and looked like she could very well qualify for any college athletic team. But she was also a highly trained and disciplined musician. Her long arms and fingers were a dead giveaway. The Tiger Crew members trying to keep up with her were mesmerized by her rhythm and motions to the music. All of this excitement kept their hearts beating at an above-normal rhythm. She alone was an incentive and motivation to keep moving and working. The captain had warned Ginger and Julie to take it slow, lest one of the out-of-shape dads or grandpas should suffer a heart attack or stroke. At the present time there was no way the Michigan would be able surface for emergency care. It had its own emergency—a national one.

Julie was in a bad mood. David could sense it almost immediately, and he thought he knew what the problem was. It was stress and worry—and possibly one other reason. At a break during the midpoint of the session while they were alone and all of the other participants were out of the area getting a drink of water or visiting the bathroom, David asked Julie, "Is everything okay this morning, Julie?"

"Why wouldn't it be?" she snapped back.

"I don't know," David answered. "You don't seem to be your jovial self this morning."

The Tiger Cruise

"How would you know?" she snapped again.

David just stood looking at her, not saying anything. *She's not in the mood to comment rationally,* he thought. After a minute, David handed her his cold water bottle. "Here, take a drink of water. This will cool you off." He unscrewed the sealed water bottle and handed it to Julie. She gulped it down angrily with some of it spilling onto her face, neck, shoulders and finally onto her gym suit. A few drops ended up on the floor of the Michigan. David bent down and wiped them up with a towel.

"Thank you," she said quietly but hastily.

David remained quiet for the next few moments while Julie leaned up against a nuclear silo tube with her eyes closed. David just kept looking at her, trying to burn her image into his mind forever. Someday, this memory would come back to him when he listened to a CD of her performing a piano concerto with a major symphony orchestra. He was sure this would happen.

The aerobics class participants soon returned from their break, and Julie started the music once again. She was still in an unpleasant state of mind. Most of the other members of the class also sensed the apparent change in Julie's demeanor. They looked at David, at each other, and finally at Julie.

When the class was done at about 6:30, David stayed around purposely until he and Julie were the only ones remaining.

"I'm sorry I snapped at you, David," she said apologetically. "Maybe it's the pressure building on me. I sometimes get this way when I have a concert or recital on my mind. And I'm not even certain that we're going to make it to the surface in time."

"I understand," David said empathetically. "Even I get that way at times. Here, let me give you a back rub. Maybe it will relax you." He didn't wait for Julie to give him permission to do it—he knew what he was about to do may leave him on the receiving end of a punch thrown by someone who had arms and hands as strong as any sailor on the Michigan. He just reached around Julie with his long arms, pulled her toward him, and began to rub her shoulders gently with his long, strong fingers. He massaged her shoulder blades and worked down her back. He could feel she was tense and how the rubdown was relaxing her. He worked his hands and fingers all over

The Tiger Cruise

her back for at least a minute. He would have continued for ten minutes more were it not for the sound of someone coming up the stairs. What if it was the captain or the COB? What if it was a sailor that liked to spread rumors and get other sailors into trouble?

Julie quickly grabbed onto David and gave him a firm hug. He could feel her strength.

Julie and David quickly let go of each other and reached for their jackets. By the time the sailor saw them, they were already walking in opposite directions.

As Julie walked to her room she felt relaxed—ready to eat breakfast and practice her felt piano for the rest of the morning. She also started to have a feeling for David that countered the hostility she sometimes had toward him.

David, more than ever, saw Julie as someone he wanted to get to know more. But something inside him told him to be careful—for many reasons.

At 7:00 a.m. the Great Lakes Café was unusually busy. The only table available when Ginger and Julie had gotten their breakfast was the one where David was once again sitting by himself. Ginger started walking toward the table, then hesitated, seeing that Julie had not moved. Julie wanted to find two empty tables to accommodate her fake keyboard in order to practice after she had finished breakfast. Her eyes scanned the room, hoping to find a spot. She finally gave up and followed Ginger to David's table. They sat down and began eating.

"Did you girls have a good workout?" David asked, trying to start a conversation in a pleasant manner. "I'm all ready to take on whatever the Navy orders me to do today."

"I was up most of the night," Ginger responded, "I'm not feeling all too well this morning. Maybe it's something I ate last night."

David, trying to give her some comfort, responded, "That happens even on the Michigan."

There was a short interval of silence while the three were busy eating their food. Suddenly, Julie turned to David and said, "Thank you for the short back rub. It relaxed me, but don't read too much into it." She then turned her attention back to her meal.

The Tiger Cruise

David was surprised she mentioned anything about it in front of Ginger, but responded, "You're welcome. Anytime."

Julie then left the mess hall.

Ginger was surprised at Julie's comment. "What was that all about?" she asked David. "And what was the 'don't read too much into it' all about?"

"I just helped her relax a little bit with a very short back rub," he answered. "I'm not sure what she meant by that statement."

Ginger looked at David with her mouth open. "That's interesting," she responded. "And she didn't haul off and slug you?"

David smiled at Ginger and answered, "I think she enjoyed it."

After the noon meal, the mess hall was busy with activity. A few members of the Tiger Crew met in one corner for a game of gin rummy. The three divorced dads sat alone plotting their next move in their ongoing legal cases. Their stories changed every day and became more incredible. Their divorce settlements were not complete, and it would be months before all of the appeals were exhausted. Many of the rest of the Tiger Crew were engaged in book reading or in conversations with some of the sailors. The remainder headed for their assigned duties.

Julie was also busy playing her felt piano on the room's one long table. Sailors were sitting at adjacent tables watching her— not exactly interested in the music of Rachmaninoff, but in Julie herself. Some of the sailors, though, were actually starting to enjoy Rachmaninoff's music. As she was practicing, she continued to wonder how she got the keyboard, CD player, headphones and music. It was all too much of a coincidence. Her parents could have managed to get them on the sub during one of the surfacing exercises, she thought, but there had been no surfacing exercises or any contact with the mainland. She was starting to have a pretty good idea of who was responsible, however.

At the evening meal, the Tiger Crew had a big surprise when Alex Perkins walked into the mess hall with his son and announced, "Hey, guys, guess what! I've been healed!" The entire Tiger Crew looked at Alex and wondered what he was talking about. For a

The Tiger Cruise

moment, most of the crew tried to remember what Alex's problem was. What had he been healed of? When they saw that he was not picking up paper off of the floor or wiping the edges of the table, they suddenly remembered that he had suffered from Obsessive Compulsive Disorder.

One person who understood Alex's condition—or now his previous condition—was Dr. Dave Simmons. He stood up and walked over to Alex, very interested in what had taken place. "I studied this mental malady when I was in medical school, and I became very interested in it. Let's see if you truly no longer have it, Alex."

Dr. Dave, who had operated on hundreds of heads and other parts of the human body, took two pieces of a paper mat sitting on the table and crumpled them into balls. Then he threw them onto the floor. "Pick them up Alex!" Dave commanded.

Alex responded, "Pick them up yourself. I'm not a janitor."

A great cheer went up from everyone in the mess hall.

"What happened to him, Doc?" Max Schroeder asked.

"Most likely when Alex hit his head and was knocked unconscious, whatever was causing his OCD must have reversed itself and he is now okay. Actually, I don't have a clue of what happened, but something must have snapped back. I hope the reversal is permanent and not just a temporary fluke."

Alex's son gave his dad a big hug. Alex responded. "Wait until your mother hears about this. Maybe now she'll take me back."

Shortly after 8:00 p.m., David saw Julie coming toward him in the hall outside the mess hall. She was with her escort. "Hi, Julie," David said. He wanted to say more to her, like, "Can we go out on a date sometime?" but he was waiting for the right time to ask. Maybe the time was right. *Why not?* he thought. He held his breath as he waited to see how she responded to his greeting.

"Hi, David. What's up?"

"I am off tonight. Would you like to meet me for coffee in the Great Lakes Café?"

"I would like that," she answered. "What time?"

"How about in fifteen minutes?"

"Sounds good," she said. Her answer took him by surprise. It was only the second time he had asked a girl on a date. The other time was when the Michigan had stopped in Singapore and he had a three-day pass. He had found a small church on Sunday morning and had been invited over to the pastor's house for lunch. The pastor had a twenty-year-old daughter. Dave asked the daughter to accompany him to a movie that night.

At 8:20 David and Julie met at a table in the corner of the Great Lakes Café. Since this was David's idea, he decided to take the lead in the conversation. "You know, Julie, this is a first."

"First what?" Julie asked.

"This the first time a sailor and a beautiful young lady have had a formal date on this submarine — let alone any sub. Women are not allowed to serve on submarines in the US Navy."

"I never thought of it. I believe you are correct," Julie responded.

David leaned across the table, lowered his voice, and whispered to her, "I must warn you that we could be interrupted at any time by one of the officers or even the good Captain Wagner."

"Why would that be?" Julie asked with a puzzled expression.

"I think they have been advised to be on the lookout for anything that resembles romantic behavior involving you girls," David answered. "So if any of the chiefs, officers, or Captain Wagner approaches us while we are talking, just follow my lead. Okay?"

"Okay," Julie answered.

David quickly changed the subject. "Now, let's talk about something that we agree on."

"Good idea. So what do we agree on?"

David thought about it for a moment and responded, "I'll pick a subject and then you pick one. How about music?"

"Sounds good, I believe that's something we do agree on," Julie said.

Just then one of the chiefs walked up to them and stood next to the table they were sitting at. David immediately started talking. "As a matter of fact, the Michigan has a length of almost two football fields and a width forty-two feet."

The Tiger Cruise

Julie broke in, "You've got to be kidding me! She is one big puppy, ain't she?"

"You know what else?" David responded in a clear voice, wanting the chief especially to hear him.

"What?" Julie asked.

"The Michigan has the best chiefs in the U.S. Navy ... Oh, hi, Chief Anderson." The chief just rolled his eyes and walked away. David turned to Julie and whispered, "Our coffee date has been salvaged."

The discussion then turned back to the agreed topic—music.

"Julie, have you ever played the Rack 3?" David asked.

"Yes," she answered. "That's the next concerto I'll perform, probably in the next two years."

"Question," David said with a sense of hesitation. "Which concerto is the hardest to perform?"

Julie suddenly realized that David's knowledge of music was more than she first thought. She thought for a moment and then answered, "For the pianist, it's the Rack 3. For the orchestra, it's the Rack 2."

For the next hour, Julie and David talked about music and their careers. It was a time of getting to know each other in a positive way. Both of them steered away from the topics that would turn the discussion negative.

Just prior to 11:00 p.m. Jake Johnson sent a message to both his mom and dad requesting that they have lunch with him the next day. He had decided it was time for them to get together and discuss reconciliation. Soon he received a written reply. Both agreed to the meeting.

Ginger passed David in the hall and quietly said to him, "I'm curious about this back rub business that Julie mentioned at breakfast this morning."

"I gave her something to relax her this morning after the aerobics class and after you and everyone else left," David answered. "I felt she needed it and I didn't even ask her."

"I was wondering what took her so long to come back to our room," Ginger added. "Didn't she mind? You might have gotten slugged for even touching her."

"I think she enjoyed it ... but I was ready to be slugged, also," he responded.

"You know, David," Ginger said thoughtfully, "I think she likes you. And at the same time, I think she hates you. It doesn't add up. What do you think, David?"

"The problem can be summed up with one answer. Julie has a spiritual issue," David answered.

"Well," Ginger responded, "let me tell you something. Everyone on the Michigan talks about Julie; but when I am talking to her at night, you're the only person on this boat she talks about. It's not always positive talk, but it's talk."

* * * * *

It was just prior to midnight in the command center. The opinion of all those present was that the Lost Sub Crisis was beginning to become critical, and it had to be resolved soon. The sub was no doubt North Korean since their government refused to talk about losing one—especially one that was supposedly high tech. Captain Wagner was ready to take some decisive action.

Chapter 8

The Tiger Cruise—Day 7—Tuesday

The two school teachers on the Tiger Crew were in the mess hall drinking coffee at 5:00 a.m. Joe Rosenberg had taught history at various levels, including junior and senior high in the Brooklyn school system, Jewish history in a Hebrew school in Brooklyn, and world history at the college level. Alex Perkins had taught high school social studies in Boise, Idaho, until his nervous breakdown. These two navy dads had conversed several times about their sons in the past few days, but not about their professions. Joe was well aware of Alex's OCD disability and respected him by not asking questions that were too sensitive. Now that he was apparently functional again, he felt confident the conversation could be more open.

"How did you like teaching history?" Alex asked.

Joe was both surprised and happy for the question. He wanted to talk shop. He quickly answered, "I loved it at the college level. Those kids wanted to learn ... at least most of them. My answer is different for the junior and senior high school level. Much of my time was spent disciplining the bratty kids with very little help and support from their parents. The teaching of Jewish history I found somewhat boring since I am not a religious person. In fact, my father was an atheist. He never observed the Jewish holidays." Joe took a slow sip of coffee then asked, "How about your teaching, Alex? Did you like it?" Joe was a little hesitant asking the question of Alex, as it could open old wounds.

The Tiger Cruise

"Actually, I also loved teaching," Alex answered, "but in my case, the kids finally got to me. That's when I acquired my nervous condition. Maybe I'll go back to it when we surface."

"So what did you teach?" Joe asked him.

"Mostly high school social studies. I also taught some math and science whenever the school was short of a teacher for those subjects. My ambition was to teach at the college level, but that wasn't to be." They both stopped talking at that point and just drank their coffee. Both of these navy dads had two things in common: education and their U.S. Navy offspring.

It seemed everyone on the Michigan was in love with Julie. She was the sweetheart of the USS Michigan. What else could be expected from a multitude of young—and even some old—sailors returning from a seventy-seven day cruise around the Pacific Ocean? Hormones were going wild, and there was still no end in sight for this particular cruise.

The mood in the mess hall spelled trouble right from the start of breakfast. Julie and Ginger walked in and got in line to get their breakfast. They found a table with three empty chairs in about the center of the room. Joey Wagner, the captain's son who was part of the Tiger Crew, occupied the third chair, leaving an empty seat next to Julie. David was already seated just one table away. Two sailors coming off of the serving line both saw the empty seat next to Julie. David knew exactly what would happen next. Both of the sailors spotted the empty chair and quickly lunged forward to fill it.

There had been discussions among the chiefs and some of the officers as to the negative aspect of Julie's presence on the sub. "There's bound to be a dog fight at some point—it will eventually get out of control and someone will get hurt," one of the chiefs had said.

David was through eating and watched the scene unfold from where he was seated. The noise level was quite high and was about to get higher. One of the two sailors managed to place his tray on the table first, while the other sailor began to sit down. The two of them suddenly faced each other. Words were exchanged and open hands soon became fists. David had witnessed fights form and accelerate quickly numerous times, and he knew that was what was

The Tiger Cruise

about to transpire. He thought about Julie having to explain to one of the officers her involvement in a fight in which sitting by her was the prize. Also, thinking about Julie's safety—especially her valuable arms and hands—David quickly jumped up and took two steps to where Julie was sitting. From behind her, he grabbed Julie around her stomach, chair and all, and pulled her out of the way. The fighting sailors crash-landed on the floor where Julie had been sitting. As the sailors proceeded to fight on the floor, everyone close by stood up and got out of the way. Tables and chairs tipped over, dishes and food landed on the floor, and the clean and well-pressed navy clothes became wrinkled and soiled. The conflict lasted for about twenty seconds until wiser sailors stepped in and pulled them apart. Once that happened, the two sailors cooled down and realized that they had just made fools out of themselves. Fortunately, there were no chiefs or officers present. Everyone knew why they were fighting. They spent the next five minutes cleaning up the floor, repositioning the tables and chairs, and shaking hands.

Meanwhile, Julie was not immediately aware who had saved her from getting crushed by 350 pounds of U.S. Navy personnel, but she was frightened and suddenly lost her appetite. Within a few minutes everything was back to normal. It was the first time ever that any boys had fought over Julie.

So far all of the Tiger Crew members were performing their assigned jobs at the times indicated on the chart posted outside the mess hall. The system was working well. Some of the dads were even learning new jobs. The investment-minded dads were beginning to talk about how they were going to invest their Navy paychecks.

Four of the dads were together in the mess hall discussing their investments. A stock market report had not been received since the first day of the emergency because there was no satellite transmission. They could only imagine and speculate what was happening on Wall Street. Maybe this would be a good day, the four dads hoped.

The efficiency of the Tiger work crew had increased to the point where the chief in charge was having difficulty finding enough work for all aboard. He was beginning to wish the extended cruise

The Tiger Cruise

would soon end. What had started out as being five hours of work each day for each of the dads had decreased to about four hours. The extra guard and watch duty needed with the emergency on the Michigan was made easier to schedule because of all the extra help. Another benefit was that the Tiger Crew work detail kept the navy dads from getting bored and from playing too much poker in the Great Lakes Café.

The day's duty roster indicated that Julie was scheduled to help out in the kitchen from 1:00 p.m. until 5:00 p.m. It was a stroke of good fortune for David, for he was to be the person who would work beside her, train her, and answer any questions she had. Whether this was intentional on the part of the chief putting the list together or just a happy coincidence, David was not certain. He just accepted it as an opportunity to get to know Julie more. On the other hand, it may not be a good thing—they may get to know each other too well.

David showed up early in the kitchen, and Julie walked in two minutes before 1:00. The noon meal had just been served, and it was time to begin preparation of the evening meal. Everything needed to be prepped and put in storage pans, then placed in the cooler. The work to be done by David and Julie was to prepare the items for the evening salad bar.

"Are you already to go to work?" David asked Julie.

"I am," she answered, "but I'm not sure what I am to do. You realize, don't you, that I have had little or nothing in the way of training in the culinary arts."

"Not to worry," David responded, "neither did I when I enlisted in the Navy about eighteen months ago. Now I am going to train you."

"I just hope I don't poison anyone with my work," Julie said. After a slight pause she added, "There's one thing I want to tell you before I start. Please don't preach to me about your faith and religion. Okay?"

David looked at Julie for a moment and said nothing. Her comment was somewhat expected by David, but still disappointing.

"Don't worry, Julie," David responded, "this is going to be strictly the culinary arts. If you will permit me, I do have one thing I am going to tell you from the start," David said insistently.

The Tiger Cruise

"What's that?" Julie asked in an apprehensive tone.

"I don't want you to use any knives in cutting up vegetables," David answered. "Neither do your fans in the music world. Let's just say I want to protect your pretty valuable hands from being accidentally cut. They are both pretty hands and valuable hands."

"That's thoughtful of you David," Julie responded, "but that's not necessary ... or is it?"

"Well," David answered, "whether or not it's necessary, that's what we're going to do ... or, rather, not do."

Julie looked at David and said in an apologetic tone of voice, "David, I'm sorry about my religion comment. I don't know what made me say that. Forgive me."

"Forgiven! We're going to get along just fine," he said.

"So, what exactly are we going to do?" she asked.

David answered by setting a lettuce shredder in from of her. "I will trim the heads of lettuce and place them in front of you. You put them in the hopper and turn the handle. The shredded lettuce will come out the end and into the stainless steel pans. When the pans are full, just cover them with this plastic wrap and set them on that table there," he said pointing to the table behind them.

For the next hour, Julie and David cut lettuce, cabbage, and carrots. Then it was on to opening and emptying cans of various other ingredients that would make up the salad bar—not only for the Tuesday-evening meal, but also for the next two days. By 3:00 p.m., the work was done. David could have excused Julie to go back to her quarters, but he decided to find something to occupy her for as long as he could.

"Julie, is there anything that you would like to make here in the kitchen?" he asked.

"Actually, there is," she answered. "I would like to make some cookies. I have never made any cookies. I really want to make some chocolate chip cookies. Can we do that, David?"

"We can do that, Julie," David answered. He opened a cupboard and selected a Better Homes and Gardens cookbook. He went to the index and turned to the page that had a recipe along with a picture of chocolate chip cookies. "Let's make these. Do they look good to you?"

The Tiger Cruise

"Yes, they do," she answered.

David set the ingredients, the measuring utensils, and the recipe in front of Julie. "Go to it, Julie," he said in a confident voice. "Just follow the instructions in the recipe."

She looked at David with a doubting stare. "What happens if I make a mistake?" she asked.

"Don't worry, I'll watch you closely," David answered.

"Isn't that what you've been doing for the past few days?" she asked.

David stopped for a moment, looked at her, then answered, "I didn't think you noticed. I do know that all of the other sailors have been looking at you, also."

"I know that too," she responded, "but you especially. I think you have a thing for me."

"Well, start the cookies!" David responded, attempting to get her back on track.

Julie proceeded to make cookies for the first time. Her mother had never taken the time to show her how, nor could Julie afford the time between piano lessons, practice, and school, to learn how to do any kind of cooking. But today she was doing it.

While she was making the cookies, David thought of something that had him puzzled. "Julie, you have long hair. How come you never wear it down?"

Julie kept working as she answered David's question. "I guess it's easier to manage if I wear it up on top of my head."

"Can you wear it down sometime before we surface, so I can see you with it long? David requested.

"Maybe," Julie answered.

Within forty-five minutes, the smell of freshly baked cookies permeated that entire section of the USS Michigan. Everyone close by came in to help themselves to at least one of them. David set aside six of them, then he placed two of them on a paper plate and covered it with plastic wrap. He put the paper plate in Julie's hand, took her other hand in his, and led her out of the kitchen and into the hallway.

"Where are you taking me?" she asked.

The Tiger Cruise

"Just be patient and follow me, "David answered. He led her up the section of stairs to the command center. Soon they approached Captain Wagner's quarters—the same place the guards had led Julie and Ginger on the first day of the cruise. David knocked on the closed door, and a moment later the captain opened the door.

"What do we have here? Ah! A plate of freshly baked cookies! I wondered where that familiar smell was coming from." The captain quickly removed the wrapping and consumed the two cookies in less than a minute's time. "Wonderful! And who baked them?"

"Julie did, Captain," David answered as she grinned.

"Thank you, Julie," the captain said. "Your talent extends beyond just playing the piano. I think these have extra chocolate chips and nuts ... just the way I like them."

"You're welcome, Captain," responded Julie. "David suggested we double the nuts and chips in the recipe." With that they went back to the kitchen.

"We've got an hour left on my shift," Julie said. "What do I do now?"

David thought about it and answered, "Well, I am in charge of you, so I could dismiss you. Or we could find some other work in the kitchen. So I guess it's up to you. You can go to your quarters and get some beauty sleep, or we can stay here and just talk."

Julie looked at David and smiled. She knew what he wanted to do. Her answer came as a complete surprise to David. "Let's each ask one question that will require a long answer."

He quickly responded, "We'll flip a coin to see who goes first." He took a Michigan battle coin that he had in his pocket and flipped it into the air. As it landed in his hand, he covered it with his other hand. "Call it, Julie."

"Heads," she said.

"Heads it is. What's your question?"

Julie thought a moment and then asked, "What do you plan to do with the rest of your life?"

David stared at Julie, attempting to understand the reason for her question. It was a question that was always on his mind. Most sailors think about it since for most of them the navy is a temp job until they get out. Finally he took a deep breath and began to answer.

The Tiger Cruise

"Well, interesting you should ask me that question. I ask myself that question almost every day. There are several options I have in mind ... maybe a naval career, maybe a businessman, or maybe a teacher. I don't really know." He stopped and looked down for a moment, then looked back at Julie. "This may upset you, but to me the critical question is: What does God what me to do with my life?"

Julie quickly interrupted, "That's silly! Why does that matter? Can't we do what we want?"

David waited a moment before he responded, "Isn't that what most people do anyway?"

"Yeah ... I suppose," Julie responded.

"Then the question becomes: Are those people happy in what they're doing?" David asked.

"Maybe ... maybe not," Julie responded. "Okay. Here is an add-on question: What is happiness?"

David started wondering where this discussion was going. He thought he knew. "There are probably as many answers to that question as there are people." David replied.

"But what is it to you, David?"

"Well, let's see now ... that's about four questions that you've asked."

Julie smiled in an apologetic manner.

"I think people are happy when they are satisfied with what they have."

"Are you happy being on this submarine, being in the navy, with not much to look forward to in life?"

David was a little taken aback by Julie implying that the navy didn't give him much to look forward to.

"I don't think I would say I don't have much to look forward to. You may not agree, but in the end the happiest people in the world are those who are doing what God wants them to do—maybe in doing some work that helps people."

Julie frowned and said, "I don't think I agree with you, David. I think happiness is doing what you want to do." David decided that the discussion had gone far enough. To go any further would be fruitless. He needed to give an exit comment.

"Well, like I said, there are as many answers to the question of what happiness is as there are people." Just then the kitchen door opened and David was called out for a meeting.

David did not get the chance to ask his question of Julie. *Someday I might,* he hoped.

Ginger and her ex-husband, ex-navy chief Warren Johnson, along with their son Jake, had asked Captain Wagner to meet with them to discuss a special topic. Jake had given his notes to his mom and dad; and after a lengthy discussion, they had asked to meet with the captain. They sat in a quiet corner of the Great Lakes Café.

"So what do you wish to talk about, Warren?" the captain began. "You called the meeting." All were sipping on their cups of coffee or tea.

Warren said, "Ginger and I want to get remarried." He was noticeably nervous as he started to speak but quickly regained his composure. "In fact, my son Jake, here, was the one who really pushed it. But Ginger and I have discussed it at length, and we want to also. As captain of this boat, we want you to remarry us. And we want to do it on top of the Michigan just before Ginger departs for home ... if we ever surface. Can we do it?"

The captain smiled and responded, "Well, this is a surprise ... and, then again, it isn't. I halfway expected this would happen after watching you two together for the past seven days. Jake and I have had several discussions on this very topic in the past several months. It is clear to me that you are serious about this matter, also. What woman would risk the consequences of disrupting a United States nuclear submarine without a good reason? I think I have a marriage ceremony outline in my office for such an occasion as this. It isn't the first time it's been done, you know."

"Thank you, Captain. We really appreciate it," responded Ginger.

"You both realize, of course, that you will no doubt have an audience, in addition to the sailors on the top."

"Who else is going to be there?" asked Warren.

Captain Wagner again broke out with a big smile and answered, "Well, let's see, now. You'll likely have some families at the dock

The Tiger Cruise

waiting for the sub. Next, the press will try to get as close as possible, but they will not be allowed on the base. They have been reporting any news—or 'non-news'—about us ever since the explosions on the first day. And, of course, our sailors will be there. We'll most likely be surrounded by a navy escort of some sort. Who knows ... maybe our pianist, Julie, will have her family in attendance. But, then again, it may not happen. She may be gone by that time."

* * * * *

David was asleep on his bunk when he was awakened by one of the chiefs. It was late and David was tired. The chief spoke quietly so that no one would hear him. "David, the captain wants to talk to you. Can you come quickly?" Within two minutes David was dressed and on his way toward the command center.

"What up?" David inquired with great curiosity.

"I have no idea," the chief answered, "something important enough to get him to stop a meeting with his officers and chiefs and to get you out of a deep sleep."

They kept quiet as they climbed up two sections of stairway until they came to the chiefs' eating quarters. David walked in and the chiefs left. David saluted the captain. "You asked for me, sir?"

"Yes, I did. Shut the door and have a seat." The commander poured two cups of coffee and placed one in front of David. "David, you have a high security clearance and what I am about to tell you is of that nature. You, I and three other personnel onboard the Michigan are the only people that will know what we will be discussing here. You understand then that this is highly secret information?"

"Yes I do, sir."

"I would like to pick your brain. Remember the other night when you voiced a theory about our tagalong North Korean sub, and you suggested that this may be a bunch of North Korean sailors who may just want to escape to the west?"

"Yes, sir. I do remember."

"Well, I believe you may be correct. It appears to be the only logical answer. This thing has got us stumped. The sub keeps following us from a short distance, and yet they do not answer any

The Tiger Cruise

of our sonar contact attempts. They aren't attempting to contact anyone else either—not even their own navy or government. It's almost as if the sub is just floating in the water with no one aboard. But it still wants to stay with us wherever we go. I believe they know we are going to protect them from their own navy.

"We assume the sub is armed with torpedoes, and whoever is onboard will use them if anyone tries to attack it; but we don't know that for sure. Furthermore, they know that we do not want to risk starting a war and will not attack them. There are several unanswered questions, like: What do they want? How did they get here? How did they escape from their North Korean base? What are their intentions? Are they part of a spy mission?" Captain Wagner paused.

"Sir, what kind of a sub is it?" David asked.

"We haven't seen it, but our sonar crew says it's about the same size as our Indianapolis-class fast-attack subs," the captain answered. "We think it's a new type of submarine that the North Koreans have developed—probably nothing technologically unique. We also suspect it may be a spy sub or even a dummy sub just to annoy our navy."

David was waiting to voice his opinion but wanted the captain to finish first.

"We have had no contact with the Navy, but my guess is the pressure is building to conclude this crisis. The Navy, myself, and the U.S. government all want this over." The captain paused and was anticipating some response. "David, what wild ideas do you have in your mind?"

David's thoughts were well-organized and he was ready to offer his suggestions. "Well, sir, let's assume for starters that there is a group of young sailors on that sub who want to defect to the West—for whatever reasons. Maybe they just want to be free." David stopped at this point to let the captain soak up his main assumption—one that had been forming in David's mind and was finally being verbally expressed. The captain folded his hands and looked directly at David.

"Okay. So then what?"

"I've given this much thought," David answered. "First of all, we need to contact someone on that sub to let them know we're friendly and mean them no harm. We need to determine what they

The Tiger Cruise

are trying to do and what they want. Tell me, Captain, are the North Koreans after them?"

"Before we submerged, we had several satellite reports of a group of North Korean submarines that were headed for the West Coast of the United States." answered the captain.

"For what reason?" David asked.

"No one knows," the captain answered, "but my guess is they are trying to catch their runaway submarine."

David was quick to reply, "That is just what happened in *The Hunt For Red October*. Remember?"

"Indeed I do," replied the captain.

"Someone from this sub needs to make contact with the tagalong," David suggested in a slightly raised voice.

"How do we do that?" Captain Wagner asked.

"We go over, knock on their door and ask them directly," was David's no-nonsense answer.

The captain looked at David for a moment and then said, "And get shot by a North Korean sailor using a Russian handgun? Are you crazy?"

David covered his face with his hands.

"David, I believe your analysis. I'm buying it, hook, line, and sinker," the captain said.

David quickly uncovered his face and said to the captain, "Look, the youth are much the same in any country. They are somewhat daring, adventuresome, and rebellious. You are well aware of that, Captain. At one time I was like that, and the Navy drove it out of me."

The captain suddenly changed the look on his face from a somewhat negative expression to one where he was definitely in agreement with his young enlisted Michigan sailor. David continued, "There may even be a few older sailors on that sub—maybe even a chief or two or three. For sure, one of the sailors on board is the leader or organizer of the mutiny. He is the one we need to make contact with."

Both the captain and David up until this time had been sitting. The captain suddenly stood up and took a sip of the cold coffee he was drinking. He was quiet for a while then said, "You're not making this story up as you go along, are you?"

The Tiger Cruise

"No. But I will tell you this." David lowered both his head and voice as he seemed to not want anyone else to hear him. "Before I walked in here, I prayed that God would give me wisdom and boldness as I spoke to you. I also asked God to give you great wisdom in the decision that you alone are about to make."

Captain Wagner looked at David and responded in an equally lowered voice, "I know that you are a very religious person. That's one of the reasons I trust you. Here is one more question before I dismiss you. If you were in command, what would you do with the North Korean submarine?"

"Simple. I would turn the boat over to Navy Intelligence to examine and then fake an explosion ... something similar to what happened in *Red October*. The North Koreans won't care about their lost sailors. They'll just be happy that their new sub didn't get into the hands of the U.S. Navy ... or so they'll think."

"Thank you for coming to see me at such a late hour. We'll probably be in further contact," the commander said. David knew what the captain meant. At that point David left.

As he lay in bed, David wondered what was going to happen next. The lost sub crisis had to be resolved in the next two days for a number of reasons.

Chapter 9

The Tiger Cruise—
Day 8—Wednesday

David was in the Great Lakes Café by 4:00 a.m. He talked the chief cook into making him a pot of flavored coffee and giving him a freshly baked caramel roll from the kitchen. He wanted to write a note to Julie and either give it to her in person or have Ginger give it to her. It would contain just exactly what was on his mind and how he felt about her. He knew what he wanted to say—he just needed to put it down on paper. It would be at least two hours before the Michigan crew and the Tiger Crew would begin to enter the mess hall for breakfast, and he wanted to write in peace and quiet.

Before he even had a sip of his coffee or a bite of the roll, he bowed his head and prayed. *Lord, give me the exact words to write in this letter to Julie. I have prayed about it and have spoken to You often. Now I want to write what's on my mind and in my heart, but at the same time I wish to do Your will. Amen.*

David looked up and noticed that two of his fellow sailors had just walked in and were getting their coffee. He began to consume his coffee and roll. The roll was dripping with thick, hot caramel. After smearing it with butter, eating it required the use of either a fork or a spoon—sometimes both. This food was definitely not for the Michigan Fat Dads. After eating the roll he began to write.

Dear Julie,

It's possible that I may not see you again, at least on the Michigan. So I want to write this note to you to tell you how I feel about you.

I am torn between two passions, my love for God and my love for you. I desire to do what God wants me to do. On the subject of God you and I are not in agreement. Something says to me, "Do not go any further with Julie." But I cannot get my mind off of you. I take this as a sign—a sign that God's purpose will be served in a relationship with you—at least for the duration of this cruise and maybe into the near or far future. I have no idea what's going to happen, but I know it could be big and wonderful.

I would like to have lunch with you and talk to you before we leave the sub. This may not be possible, however. I may have a very important assignment in the next couple of days. I would like to get your address where I can write to you. Please give Commander Wagner your address only if you wish. If you don't wish to, I will understand. If nothing else, I want to follow your career as I love the same music as you do. I want to see you and hear you perform someday in the future.

If I don't get to hear from you again, I want to wish you a happy and fulfilled future. Thank you for reading this letter.

Love, David Cordell.

PS—What I am really saying is that I have fallen in love with you on this cruise.

David folded the letter, placed it into an envelope, and sealed it.

****

Because the Michigan was at the final stages of its run, a few of the sailors were worried about who they would meet at the parking lot on their return. Would it be their wife and family or would it be their wife's lawyer with divorce papers? It had happened on numerous occasions to returning sailors. Being gone at sea for seventy-seven days was not the best thing for family life and especially a new marriage. There were no direct communications with the family, other than a family-gram sent by satellite.

* * * * *

Up in the control room the sonar people were busy with strange responses from the Michigan's main objective, the runaway North Korean sub. The sonar chief was smiling as Captain Wagner approached the sonar desk and sat down. "I'm hearing music," he said, "and not just music that you would think. Would you believe we are hearing 'American country Western cheatin' music'?"

Captain Wagner gave a frown, looked at the sonar chief, and said, "Has that music gotten into the Korean culture too? Just keep monitoring the sub and keep me informed."

* * * * *

The breakfast that morning was one of the best served on the Michigan. It was pancake morning—a favorite among the sailors. There were also link sausages and grapefruit. The Michigan kitchen staff was expecting an early crowd. The food cooler was getting low. If the Lost Sub Crisis wasn't resolved in a few days, food might have to be rationed. The extra seventeen people on this particular cruise was taking its toll on the food situation. The original Tiger Cruise was only supposed to last two days. It was now day eight.

By mid morning, several of the Tiger Crew had convened in the mess hall and asked Jimmy Runsaway about the origin of his last name. He had promised to tell the story and this morning was the time. All of the crew were there, including the girls. He had everyone's attention.

Jimmy was dressed in his Native American outfit—a buffalo-skin pair of pants, a wolf-fur coat and an eagle-feathered headdress. The crowd started laughing as soon as he appeared in the mess hall. Jimmy just smiled at the crowd, turned completely around, and bowed. His grandson Geronimo just rolled his eyes when his

The Tiger Cruise

grandfather walked in. Jimmy then did a Native American dance with powwow-style singing in his Chippewa language. Applause followed.

"Here is how the story goes," he started. "I was walking in the woods on my farm near Plainfield, Wisconsin, one afternoon. It was in the early part of December, and it was at the end of mink trapping season. It had been a good year. I believe I had trapped fifty-five mink. My trapping territory covered five farms that particular season. I would give each farmer a portion of the money received at the end of the season. The prices I received that year were particularly good—$45.00 for the males and $25.00 for the females. The corn field I was strolling through had not been harvested yet, and I was unable to see much beyond the few feet in front of me.

"I knew there were wolves in the woods and corn fields because I had often seen their tracks and heard them. My eyes and ears were open for them and I had my gun ready. Suddenly, I came upon a family of wolves—mommy and daddy and five little wolves. They were in a clearing where a small pool of water had not allowed the corn seeds to germinate and grow during the spring and summer. At first the wolf family didn't hear or smell me. I stepped backward toward the path I had just come from. My boot stepped on a twig and it produced a loud 'snap!' I was suddenly noticed.

"I froze and couldn't budge. The daddy was a big one—about the size of a small pony. The mommy was especially nervous. I almost did it in my pants. I wondered what I should do—shoot, run, or lay down like I had died. If I shot my gun, the noise may bring the rest of the pack from the woods. Then for sure my days on earth would be over and I would go to the happy hunting grounds. If I lay down I may get eaten right on the spot. *Maybe I should just shoot the daddy wolf,* I thought.

"The only thing I could think of was to run. I was a fast runner back in high school on the Indian reservation and could outrun anyone in school. Of course, there were no wolves in my class in high school, so I doubted I could outrun a wolf.

"I quickly took out my knife and a big piece of summer sausage I was carrying for nourishment, and I cut it into several pieces. I then slowly laid down my gun—temporarily, of course—took off

The Tiger Cruise

my heavy coat, and then retrieved my weapon. I turned around and—Bang!—I shot my gun into the air and took off running like a scared jackrabbit. The gunshot scared the entire wolf family into seeking each other's protection for a few precious seconds.

"As I ran, I dropped the pieces of summer sausage one at a time. I ran down one row, crossed over to the next row, again down to the first row, and so on. I finally came to the ditch, on the other side of which sat my car. I ran down one side of the ditch and up the other. The front passenger-side window of my car was open, and I jumped head first through it. My head hit the opposite door and I knocked myself senseless. I don't think I was out for more than a couple of minutes. When I came to, the wolves were outside the door still chewing the sausage. My entire body was hidden from the wolves inside the car. I had run away from the wolf family! That is where I got my name Runsaway."

Geronimo was standing in back of the room and could not resist blurting out, "Granddad, that story gets more ridiculous every time you tell it!"

Everyone applauded and headed back to the coffee pots for refills.

Julie was sitting with Ginger, so David thought it would be an opportune time to give her the letter he had written earlier. He wanted to give it to her when she was alone and let her read it. Maybe Julie would respond. Ginger might even disappear so the moment would be secure for the two of them to talk.

He walked over to the table for four and sat down directly across from Julie. David glanced at Ginger and blinked. She took the hint and excused herself. The opportune moment had arrived, and he reached into his shirt pocket and pulled out the letter.

Just then, two of his sub buddies walked up to the table with their trays and sat down in the two empty seats. Julie looked at David and saw him rolling his eyes. She looked at the letter in his hand but had no idea what it was. Then she saw her name on the sealed envelope.

They all sat quietly at the table with the two sailors busy eating their meals. They were both aware of David's interest in Julie,

The Tiger Cruise

but so were others on the Michigan's crew. They sensed that they had interrupted a rendezvous between the two of them but showed little concern.

Since David was needed elsewhere in a few minutes, he could think of only one thing to do. When the two sailors were both looking down at their trays, David quietly set the letter partially under Julie's tray. Then he covered Julie's hand with his own hand and pressed it gently. David stood up, said good-bye, and walked with his tray to the mess hall disposal window. He trusted that Julie would take the letter and read it. Maybe he could discuss it later with her. He turned around and glanced at Julie. She was staring at the envelope. He suspected it may be the last time he would see her for the unforeseeable future.

* * * * *

It was just before 11:00 a.m. when David was called up to command center to meet with the captain, the COB, and the sonar chief. It was there that these three individuals formulated the plan for contacting the North Korean submarine. The captain of the Michigan had made his decision. Since there were no communications with the Navy, either directly or by satellite, the command determined they needed to make the decision based on what they knew and their own sound judgment.

David walked up the steel stairs as he had many times. This time he was a little apprehensive since he knew what the reason was. He entered the command area crammed with more than the normal number of navy personnel. Captain Wagner motioned for David to come into his office. He entered and stood quietly for a moment. There were now four people who would be witnesses to what was about to take place concerning the lost sub crisis.

The captain turned to David and gave him the news. "David, you have been selected as the one who will attempt to make contact with our North Korean friends ... or enemies ... next door. I chose you for two reasons: You are our best swimmer; but more important, you believe in this mission. Do you have any problem with that?"

The Tiger Cruise

David looked at the captain, the COB, and then the sonar chief. Then he replied, "They want to defect to America. I definitely do not have a problem with that. I will gladly do it."

The COB then commented, "As the captain said, you are the Michigan's best swimmer and the one most qualified for this mission. We don't know what the weather will be like on the surface tomorrow morning, so be prepared for anything."

"Sir," David answered, "I'm a U.S. Navy sailor and that's my job."

* * * * *

Julie was sitting alone during the dinner hour when Captain Wagner walked in. He poured a cup of coffee and, seeing Julie sitting alone, walked over and sat down across from her at the same table. "Hi, Julie," he greeted her.

She had taken a break from playing her felt piano keyboard and was sipping a cup of coffee. "Hi, Captain," she greeted him back. "Are you taking a break from driving the Michigan?"

"Yes, indeed. I do get a few of those rare moments," the captain answered with a chuckle. "I'll bet you're still busy practicing for your concert,"

"Yes, I am," Julie replied, "and, hopefully, I'll be playing it Friday evening—but maybe not. Do you think we'll soon surface, Captain?"

The captain sat silently, wondering exactly how to answer Julie's question. He could not say much for security reasons. "My advice to you, Julie," he said in a quiet tone of voice, "keep practicing." He quickly changed the topic of conversation. "Let me ask you a question."

"Sure. Fire away, Captain," Julie replied.

"How in the world did your dad acquire the last name of Furniture?"

Julie smiled and was ready to answer the same question she had answered hundreds of times before. "Good question, Captain. My great-grandfather was a furniture maker in England and was good at his trade. He was so good that people started to refer to him as 'Mr.

The Tiger Cruise

Furniture.' When he came to the United States, he decided to change his name from what it had been in England—Winter. He always told his family that he was a warm person and no longer wanted a cold name like Winter. So when he landed at Ellis Island, he changed his name to Furniture. Does that sound like a good story?" she asked with a broad grin.

"That sounds like a heck of a story, Julie," the captain answered.

Julie now wanted to ask Captain Wagner a question. "Captain, what do you think of David Cordell?"

The captain stared at Julie for a few seconds. He was well aware of David's attraction to Julie, but he wasn't sure of what Julie thought of David. Her question was an indication that she was thinking about him. He decided to give Julie a detailed answer. "David is probably the best sailor under my command at this time. But let me tell you, he wasn't always that way."

"What do you mean, Captain?" Julie inquired.

The captain thought for a moment, ran his fingers back through his hair, took a sip of his coffee, and began to answer Julie's question. "David probably wouldn't want me to tell you this, but his is a story of the navy making a fine man and sailor out of raw material. When he first came into the navy he was a little rebellious. At least that's what his records showed when he came onboard the Michigan. Then one day he asked to speak to one of the officers. In that meeting he did something that I believe no other sailor has ever done. Excuse me, Julie, while I get us a refill on the coffee. It looks like they just made a fresh batch."

Julie shifted in her chair. She wondered what the captain was going to say next. She couldn't even imagine.

When the captain returned and had placed Julie's refilled coffee cup in front of her, he continued his answer. "He met with Officer Robert Anderson and proceeded to ask the navy's forgiveness for being such a poor recruit and sailor. Officer Anderson asked David to explain what he was talking about. David told him that when he joined the navy, it was because his grandfather had just died and his dad didn't even attend the funeral. His dad was roaming the streets somewhere and did not want to settle down. There was no money

The Tiger Cruise

for David to attend college, so he joined the navy. Let's just say David was a little angry and embittered.

"David's first months in the navy tended to be an extension of his months prior to his enlistment—rebellious, bitter, and indolent. He almost got kicked out. Then one day he changed. Overnight he became the model sailor. But he regretted the time—about six months—he had wasted. His exact words were, 'I need to ask the navy to forgive me for cheating them out of doing my very best.' So, now I feel that David has a brilliant career ahead of him in the U.S. Navy ... or in whatever he does."

Julie sat quietly and seemed very interested in what the captain had to say about David.

"Julie," the Captain said, quickly changing the subject, "I imagine your arms and hands get tired when you play the piano for hours."

"Actually, it's surprising, but it's my back that produces most of the power in my playing and consequently gets tired. That is why I exercise so much."

Captain Wagner sat quietly looking at his cup. He knew what David's next task in the navy was, but he couldn't tell Julie. It was time for him to return to the control room.

Julie took the letter David had left for her back to her room. She held it in her hand for a moment and shut her eyes. She was confused as to whether or not she should open it and read it or just disregard it—destroy it. If she did not open the letter, she could go on living her life as she had prior to the Lost Sub Crisis. On the other hand, not opening the letter would rob her of ever knowing what David wanted to say to her. It was easy to see that he was very much in love with her, and she had to be honest with herself and admit that she felt the same way about him. But there was a huge difference in their career and spiritual interests.

She then thought about what David had said about taking risks in life, especially when your heart says "do it." Julie opened her eyes, tore open the envelope, and read the letter. It confirmed what she had feared, but at the same time it said what she had hoped it would.

Chapter 10

The Tiger Cruise — Day 9 — Thursday

It was exactly midnight on Thursday when the Michigan prepared to make initial contact with the North Korean sub. David began putting on his suit used by the Navy Seals. He had been trained to rescue anyone whenever it was needed. He walked over and chose the right weight of ball hammer from the maintenance shop and rigged up a holder to carry it on his waist. He also thought about what gift he could present to the sailor with whom he would first come in contact in the target sub — that is if he wasn't shot at that precise moment. He was still contemplating that decision at 4:00 a.m. when he thought of the answer. He placed in his rubber cap a postcard with a photo. If the occupants of that sub were truly desperate to go to America, they surely would recognize the photo.

Captain Wagner suddenly appeared in the maintenance shop as David was about to leave. He had come to wish David the best in what he hoped would be the conclusion of the Lost Sub Crisis. The captain had surprised David by coming. "Thank you for coming, sir. I have just one question for you. What are we calling this secret naval rendezvous?"

"How about you giving it a name, David, since you are one of the very few that has knowledge of what is about to happen?"

David was surprised, but he thought for a moment and replied, "How about if we call it 'Operation Kimchi'?".

The captain raised his eyebrows and asked, "What in the world is kimchi?" He almost immediately remembered the answer to his own question. "Oh, that's right. It's some kind of a Korean culinary."

"Exactly! It's a popular Korean dish made of rotten cabbage ... or so they tell me," David answered. "The Koreans think it's a delicacy. It smells so bad that some apartment buildings in the United States have banned the residents from cooking it."

The captain shook hands with David, gave him a hug, and left the area. Captain Wagner was one of David's heroes and looked to him as a father.

The Michigan started its slow ascent one hundred miles off the coast of Washington. Sure enough, as predicted, the North Korean submarine followed right alongside in its climb. It was as if the baby sub was staying close to its mama.

At 6:00 a.m. both subs had reached the surface, the one towering over the other above the water line. The sun was high enough to provide the right amount of light for the rare naval maneuver. The Michigan commenced to inch cautiously toward the North Korean sub. There was a slight sound throughout the Michigan as the two subs made contact. The same was true on the Kimchi. The Michigan's driver carefully kept a slight pressure on the Kimchi to maintain the physical contact. The Kimchi performed the same maneuver, causing the two subs to squeeze each other. It was like baby sub and mama sub were now cuddling each other.

David felt it and was ready but uneasy. "This is the proof that they want to defect," he said to himself.

The Michigan's crew began to open the top hatch while David stood close by on the Michigan's top level. He was trying to speculate what could go wrong in the plan mapped out earlier in the chiefs' mess hall. He was also wondering if he would ever see Julie again. She didn't know where he was or what he was doing. And she may never know. The sub crisis could be mere moments from being resolved, and she could be airlifted off the Michigan along with the other Tiger Crew members.

On the other hand, David could be shot by a North Korean sailor with a handgun, and it might start a war. But he was so confident in his theory of their intended defection that he decided to not think about something going wrong. He just silently prayed.

David said goodbye to his fellow sailors on top of the Michigan, and he jumped into the cool and calm Washington Pacific Ocean water. He quickly began swimming toward one end of the North Korean sub. Climbing on top, he crawled over to the small sub's top hatch door, kneeled down, and removed his hammer from its holder. He held it firmly and readied himself to hit the hatch door twice. *It's quiet on the sea this morning, and the sound of the impact may scare any birds nearby,* David thought to himself. A few seagulls had already landed on the top surface of the Michigan.

David placed the flat part of the hammer in the center of the steel cover. The two blows to the cover of the Kimchi's main hatch produced a muffled sound. David's heart was beating fast with a type of anxiety he had never experienced before. He quietly waited for some form of response from below the hatch cover—from whatever or whoever might be there.

As if the Kimchi's crew was anticipating the Michigan crew's every move, the door quickly opened. David stared down at a sailor staring up at him. He was a North Korean sailor approximately his same age. In his hand was a still-warm Korean eggroll on a plate. David immediately reached for the plate and proceeded to eat the eggroll like he hadn't been fed in days. "Komapsumnida. Thank you!" the American sailor said to the North Korean sailor. "Very good!"

"Annyong. Hi," the sailor greeted David.

"Annyong," David returned the greeting. He had learned the Korean greeting when the Michigan had stopped for food supplies the previous fall in South Korea. David's apparent new friend spoke in English that was clearer than expected. They looked at each other for few seconds, and then they both exchanged their names.

"I'm David," the U.S. Navy sailor said as he pointed to himself with his index finger.

"Kim," was the reply as the North Korean sailor pressed his thumb against his chest. They clasped hands firmly and shook them. David decided to make the next move.

"Kim, come." David motioned with his hand to climb up on top of the North Korean sub. Kim cautiously climbed out of the smaller sub's main hatch and stood on top.

"USS Michigan," Kim said as he pointed to the larger submarine. David was not surprised at what his new friend had just stated.

The Michigan sailors, just a few feet away with loaded concealed weapons were carefully watching. They all waved. Kim waved back. A camera sent the live encounter to a monitor sitting in the captain's quarters below. A shout of joy and a deep sigh of relief was the collective expressed response of all those gathered. The captain wondered what would happen next. The crisis was not quite over.

David made the next move. He pulled a slightly seawater-soaked postcard out of his rubber hat and gave it to Kim. "Kim, do you want to go to Disneyland in America?"

"Yes, and eleven sailors below," was Kim's answer as he pointed downward with his index finger. "Come with me." Kim motioned for David to climbed back down the hatch with him. They were soon walking down the hall and up a stairway to where the command center was located. David noticed that the sub's interior structure seemed slightly smaller than comparable U.S. fast-attack submarines.

David was wondering where Kim was taking him. Maybe it was a trap the North Korean Navy had planned from the start to take an American sailor as a hostage. David did not have a weapon, so he would be unable to defend himself. *How many other North Korean sailors are really on the sub?* David wondered.

They went to the control center of the Kimchi. There stood eleven other North Korean sailors, all with weapons at their sides ready to use if needed. David was suddenly frightened at the sight of the armed sailors but shook hands with all eleven and repeated his name to each of them. They in turn gave David their names. Kim showed the Disneyland card to each of his fellow North Korean sailors. They each made a joyful comment in the Korean language, while at the same time smiling.

David breathed a sigh of relief. The crisis was over and the next stage of the plan could now be implemented.

The Tiger Cruise

A message was immediately sent through the U.S. satellites from the Michigan that "a disabled and unmanned submarine had been discovered by the U.S. Navy and was being towed to an undisclosed location for repairs." No mention was made as to the country of origin or of any personnel inside. The Lost Sub Crisis was indeed over. Within minutes, the entire world heard the news.

* * * * *

Everyone was surprised when an announcement was made at 7:00 a.m. over the Michigan's PA system. "Attention: All Tiger Crew members please report to the mess hall for a short meeting."

It was only five minutes and the entire Tiger Crew and many of the Michigan crew had gathered in the crowded Great Lakes Café. Julie looked around for David. She walked into the kitchen area to see if he might be on duty. He was nowhere. She immediately knew that David had been involved with the resolution of the crisis. *Is he okay?* she wondered.

Captain Wagner asked for everyone's attention and began by saying, "The Lost Sub Crisis is over. 'Lost Sub' is what the entire world is calling this crisis. We are free to go home. Thank you for your patience." There was a prolonged period of cheering by both crews.

Julie made her way through the crowded room to Captain Wagner. As he saw her approaching him, he knew the question she was going to ask and rehearsed the answer quickly in his mind.

"Have you seen David, Captain Wagner? Where is he?"

The captain looked at her, placed his mouth close to Julie's ear and spoke softly in a low voice. "David is somewhere I cannot disclose at this time for security reasons. That is all I can tell you. I know that you are worried about him, but he is fine. Now, you and I never had this conversation. Okay?"

Julie and the captain stood apart and looked at each other. A tear suddenly came out of Julie's eye. "Thank you, Captain, for telling this to me."

It was determined by Captain Wagner to be safe for the Tiger Crew to make contact with their families. The Michigan had surfaced,

The Tiger Cruise

and one by one each member would be allowed to call their homes using a secured phone line via satellite.

COB Stengel explained the procedure to the Tiger Crew. "We'll take each one of you one at a time to the top of the sub where you may call your families. Make certain you have the correct phone number ready so we can dial it for you. Also, write down what you plan to say so we may approve of it. You cannot tell them where you are—other than the Pacific Ocean—or what happened. The news media has probably already done this with contrived or false information. Each member of the Tiger Crew will have two minutes of talk time. To be sure, the Navy will be listening to each call with a five second delay"

All of the families had been contacted by the Navy shortly after the cruise began on the first day. They were all worried about both their Tiger Crew family members and their navy family members on the Michigan.

The issue of the foreign sub threat had been defused without serious damage or injury, and it was now time to head for shore. They would arrive at Banger naval base within the next day. The Navy would contact each family to let them know where and at what time the sub would be docking.

Alex Perkins was most eager to talk to his family. He called his ex-wife, Emily. Her reaction when he greeted her was less than cordial. He was not expecting that, and it was very disappointing to Alex.

"Alex, is that you? Why are you calling me? Where is my son?" she asked.

Using her cell phone with the permission of Captain Wagner, Julie was able to make contact with her agent in New York City concerning her upcoming performance at the Hollywood Bowl. They were frantically trying to decide whether to cancel, postpone, or have the replacement pianist play for the concert. She asked the agent to contact her parents to tell them she was fine and not to worry about her—which she knew they would disregard. Julie's

The Tiger Cruise

parents were continually worried about her. She also told her agent that she was ready to perform the Rack 2.

* * * * *

After touring the Kimchi North Korean submarine, David and the twelve sailors came over to the Michigan where they were helped aboard by the U.S. Navy sailors. In turn, the Michigan sailors that had been stationed on the topside made their way over to the North Korean sub. None of them knew exactly what they were going to do, other than wait for instructions from the Navy and the State Department. Michigan and Kimchi crew members had tied the two subs together. The Kimchi sailors were fed a U.S. Navy meal in a restricted room on the Michigan for security reasons. In a few hours they would be secretly airlifted to an undisclosed location for a debriefing session. David would go with them.

* * * * *

It was Julie's birthday. She turned twenty years old, and the Michigan command decided to throw a submarine birthday party for her. It would be a reason to celebrate the end of the Lost Sub Crisis, the end of this Tiger Cruise, and the end of the current Pacific Rim run for the Michigan. Although at the beginning it appeared that Julie was one of the reasons the current run had been extended, she was not entirely to blame for what had happened. The Michigan and its crew had actually saved the lives of the two women involved.

The birthday party was scheduled for 3:00 p.m., and all of the personnel of the sub were invited and wanted to attend. This, of course, was impossible due to space constraints. The mess hall was not large enough to hold and serve the entire crew. For this reason, the party would need to spill over into the hall. To add to the festivities, the dinner menu would be the best of the trip: lobster, prime rib, and crab legs. The Michigan's cake decorator was doing his job on Julie's special cake, which had been baked by the kitchen cooks.

Since it would be the last full day of the Tiger Cruise, the lunch prepared by the kitchen staff was also a special one. They served

The Tiger Cruise

hamburgers made to order and American fried potatoes cooked to a golden brown on all sides. There were extra sailors placed on kitchen duty to accommodate the rush and the second helpings that would be expected. The Fat Tiger Crew Dads diet group had disbanded that morning and had already returned to their former voracious appetites. They were well on their way to regaining the few lost pounds. Most of them swore they were going to continue their diets and exercising when they returned to their homes, but not while they were still guests of the Michigan.

The Tiger Crew members were mixing in with the sailors more than usual, hoping to become better acquainted with them now that the crisis was over and they were nearly at the end of their trip.

As the two female members on the Michigan entered the mess hall, someone began to applaud and soon there was a standing ovation. The girls took a bow and laughingly acknowledged the lively acclamation. Most of the chiefs agreed that the morale of the Michigan had been greatly improved since the day the ladies had jumped on the sub. "But rest assured, the policy of not permitting women on submarines is one that will be set in concrete for a long time," the captain was overheard saying.

Julie looked around once again for David but did not see him. He had originally been assigned to kitchen duty during this lunch hour. But only the Michigan command and a small number of the crew knew what he had been doing since midnight. Julie had no idea of his important mission—only the fear of something going wrong and not seeing him again.

The Tiger Crew met at 1:00 p.m. to have a last meeting. All fifteen of the crew were in attendance, along with the two women who were the surprise add-ons. The crew became busy exchanging home and email addresses, as well as phone numbers. They also autographed ten-by-fourteen glossy photos of the Michigan and the current Tiger Crew, which would eventually hang in one of the meeting rooms. Captain Wagner and some of his chiefs were also in attendance to present Navy Achievement awards to a few members of the Michigan crew, some of whose dads were present on the sub. They would have been presented sooner had it not been for the crisis.

The Tiger Cruise

Ginger looked around for David, who was nowhere to be seen. She finally asked Julie, "Have you seen David?"

"I haven't seen him since yesterday," Julie answered. She did not say anything more, which caused Ginger to wonder. "There aren't many places he can go. Do you know where he is?" she asked.

Julie remained quiet and just shook her head. She had been asked to remain quiet. Ginger seemed to understand what was going on by Julie's facial response and silence.

Ever since Julie had received David's note to her, she had wanted to talk with him. She was sorry for the negative comments she had made to him at various times since the first day of the cruise, and she wanted to tell him that she was sorry. *I may not have a chance to see him before I leave the sub,* she thought. She hoped perhaps he would show up for her birthday party.

Ginger and Julie had made arrangements to have coffee together at 2:00 p.m. They wanted to talk about several things, including some questions Julie had about Ginger's faith. Julie had seen in Ginger a lifestyle that she desired. It was, of course, that same lifestyle she had seen in David. Ginger suspected that Julie's questions would be as much about David and his life as they would be about her own.

Julie arrived at the mess hall first and decided to write down the questions she had. Within ten minutes, Ginger joined her.

"Are you all set to play your concerto tomorrow night, Julie?" Ginger asked.

"I am," Julie answered, "thanks to someone who produced a fake piano keyboard out of nowhere."

"Let me share a little secret with you, Julie," Ginger responded. "I think I know where the fake piano came from."

"Where?" asked Julie.

"I think it was David's doing," Ginger answered.

"Really!" Julie exclaimed with surprise. "I was almost sure from the start."

"He never told me directly that it was his doing, but he did tell me in so many words," Ginger said. "He hinted to me that he knew who it was, but that I shouldn't say anything to anyone."

The Tiger Cruise

"Boy, I really need to apologize to him about a number of things. I am really sorry for how I treated David. I don't even know why I did what I did. I'm not sure if I'll ever get to see him again. I can only hope that maybe I will tomorrow morning.

"It's like the way I sometimes treated my parents. Since I am now more or less on my own, I don't do it as much ... but I was a very rebellious kid. Yet, I knew they were right in what they were telling me. The only thing that kept me from running away was my music. If it had not been for that, I would have been long gone. I need to apologize to them also."

Julie and Ginger continued to talk about related subjects and about their future. Julie was interested in Ginger's relationship with her ex-husband, Warren, and their remarriage scheduled for the next morning.

"So, Ginger, what are your plans for when you are married again? " Julie asked curiously.

Ginger was quick to respond, "Well, we'll head back to Michigan where we will have an official wedding, probably at my old church. I guess we haven't discussed that much yet. Then I will go back to work teaching, and Warren will look for some part-time employment."

Julie was ready with her next question. "What about your living apart for so many years? Isn't it going to be difficult to adjust to each other? I know from experience, watching my mom and dad."

Ginger looked at Julie and thought carefully how she should answer her thoughtful question. "The most important adjustment that Warren and I will make is to be in church the first Sunday. We'll also join a Bible study group during the week. The rest of the issues we'll probably work out one by one as they arise."

Julie did not say a word, but sat quietly in a thoughtful mode, then made a reflective observation. "I think David was right."

"About what?" Ginger responded.

"That who you marry is the second most important decision you make in life."

At 3:00 p.m. the master cook walked to their table from the kitchen carrying a birthday cake with twenty candles all lit. He had

The Tiger Cruise

to move slowly to keep the air-conditioning system from extinguishing them. Two assistant cooks came out behind him carrying two other cakes.

Within the next few minutes the mess hall was packed with officers, sailors, chiefs, and the Tiger Crew. Captain Wagner wished Julie many happy returns on behalf of the Michigan crew, and someone started singing "Happy Birthday." She stood up and thanked everyone for the cake and party. The remainder of the time was spent socializing.

* * * * *

David had wanted to give Julie a birthday present that she would remember him by. However, he was back on the North Korean submarine with three of his Michigan sailor buddies and his twelve new friends. They were headed to a secret location where all aboard would transfer to a Coast Guard boat. Another crew from Navy intelligence would take the sub to yet another secret location. From there David assumed the Navy would issue an official statement concerning the "Kimchi Affair," and the North Korean sailors would eventually be assimilated into American society. David quietly bowed his head and thanked God for protecting him and everyone on board both submarines.

* * * * *

The evening meal was a festive occasion. The sailors were anticipating their shore leave in the big city of Seattle and the surrounding area. Julie and Ginger had decided to go to bed early since they both had a big day ahead of them.

"Will you walk with me, Ginger?" Julie asked. "I want to find David. He couldn't have just disappeared."

Before they went to their room, they walked through all three floors in the areas where they were permitted to go—along with their escort guard, of course. Julie did not ask anyone about David's whereabouts. She knew he was on an important confidential assignment very few people knew about. She was hoping he might be done with the assignment and had returned, but there was no sign of him. They went back to their room. Julie did not say a word and went to bed.

Chapter 11

The Tiger Cruise—Day 10—Friday

The Michigan was back within a few miles of the Bangor submarine base at 1:00 a.m. It had arrived there on numerous occasions on its trip home from travels around the Pacific Ocean Rim and on short runs for testing purposes. This morning would be its most notable arrival at the dock because of the just-resolved Lost Sub Crisis and the resulting publicity in the news media. The weather forecast predicted a beautiful sunny Washington day. A busy morning was in store for the Michigan, its command, the sailors, and most notably the onboard Tiger Crew. The two female guests were of particular interest to the media and how they fared with over 160 males for ten days under the sea.

The Michigan's command was to the point where tempers were getting a little short, and some of them were talking a three-week leave on their return. Managing two crews and protecting the onboard female duo was about all the officers and chiefs could take. According to many of the officers, it had been a good hands-on illustration of why the Navy does not permit women on submarines.

* * * * *

The entire affair with the North Korean fast-attack submarine was now in a secret file with Navy Intelligence. It was being referred to as the "Kimchi Affair" only by those who were supposed to know.

The Tiger Cruise

Some type of information would eventually be given to the North Korean Navy Intelligence, and then the matter would be completely forgotten.

Kim and his fellow sailors would be fanned out to Korean communities around the United States and would eventually melt into everyday life. Some of them may be used by the State Department from time to time to work on their espionage program.

* * * * *

It was 1:30 a.m. and Julie had only twelve hours to get from the Michigan to where the Hollywood Bowl Orchestra rehearsed in Los Angeles. She probably would have time for only a once-through of the scheduled Friday evening concert work—the Rachmaninoff Second Piano Concerto. Then she would be off to the Hollywood Bowl where the concert was scheduled to begin at 8:00 p.m. As normal, she was nervous about the concert and had a difficult time falling asleep. She had not played on a real piano in almost two weeks. However, she felt much more confident than she had when she first came on the Michigan ten days ago.

She remembered what David had told her about the composer's trip to America on a ship to premiere his Third Piano Concerto in the early 1900s. There was no piano on board the steamship, and Rachmaninoff had to settle for a dummy silent keyboard, which he had made himself. In his case the premiere of the Rack 3 was a huge success. Julie hoped that her performance would also be a success, having practiced on a fake felt keyboard on a modern day Navy Trident Nuclear Submarine. She now knew the person responsible for providing her with the keyboard on the Michigan. *How did David put all that together?* she wondered. *Was that by chance also?* She was beginning to doubt that events happen by chance.

She had something else on her mind. For the first time in her life she had someone in love with her. David had expressed his feelings toward her in his letter. He had also expressed his doubts that a long-term relationship could ever work out because of their career choices and vocational differences. She respected him for that since it was a reality. Added to that was their religious differences. To

The Tiger Cruise

further her confusion, Julie was also in love with David and had no idea if she would ever meet up with him again. All of these concerns were producing a stressful situation for her at this time in her young career. She finally fell asleep at 2:30 a.m.

At 4:00 a.m. the Michigan was at the dock at the Bangor base. The sub was tethered securely to the dock. The first sailors out the hatch were the guards with their high-powered rifles and handguns. The Michigan—with its officers and crew—was once again back home.

Members of the Tiger Crew were seated in the Great Lakes Café drinking coffee from their insulated Michigan coffee mugs. It was hard to sleep with the anticipation of once again seeing their families. News reports were now being downloaded from satellite so that even the stock market dads had something to talk about. There had been no daily news reports since the first day of the crisis. Many belated family-grams were also being downloaded for the regular Michigan crew. Everyone was back in the normal communication mode once again.

The stillness of the submarine's improvised women's sleeping quarters was suddenly broken by a loud knock at 5:00 a.m. Julie was sound asleep. Ginger got up and slowly opened the door. It was one of their guards who had been stationed close by in the hall. "Julie is wanted by her family outside of the sub base right away," he whispered quietly.

Julie was awakened by the commotion. She quickly arose from her cot, got dressed, and said good-bye to Ginger. She grabbed her bag of Michigan souvenirs and departed the cabin quietly. With her guard leading the way, she climbed the stairs, walked past the area where she had conducted several aerobics classes, and then worked her way up the ladder to the surface of the Michigan sub. Soon she was in the parking lot where a private helicopter was waiting with her mother and father inside.

On her way from her cabin, she kept looking for David—thinking and hoping he would maybe appear. She looked on top of the sub, thinking he may be one of the security guards carrying the rifles or

The Tiger Cruise

handguns. There was no sign of him. In fact, it was almost like he had disappeared from the sub. *Could David have been a dream?* she asked herself. The entire last ten days felt like they had been a dream for her.

She thought about the two-minute back rub David had given her. She could use another one right now. She had been thinking that the concert would be canceled, or that a replacement pianist would be named and used. She wouldn't have minded if the concert had been canceled. She needed the rest her parents had scheduled for her after the concert. But the performance would be the highlight of her young career, especially now with all of the publicity.

Her parents were glad to see her. She didn't tell them about David. She would do that later.

Mom and Dad had many questions. "Are you okay?" they asked. "What about being out of practice for so many days?"

Julie had expected that question and was ready with the answer. "Don't worry, Mom and Dad, I am in practice. My arms and fingers are all set to go, and I have mastered the difficult passages."

Her parents looked at her in bewilderment and asked, "How is that possible onboard a nuclear submarine for ten days with no piano to practice on?"

"Just ask Mr. Rachmaninoff the next time you see him," Julie answered, "he'll tell you."

Julie's parents just stared at her and then each other. *What is she talking about? Has she gone stir-crazy from being trapped inside an enormous tuna can for ten days?* they wondered. *Is she hearing voices?*

Julie wondered if the Michigan was scheduled to make a stop in Hawaii during the next week or two. She would be there at the same time with her parents. She imagined David may be there, but that couldn't be since the Michigan was just returning from its Pacific run. It would be unlikely that she would even dare to contact him, especially after the manner in which she had made contact with the Michigan ten days before in the Strait of Juan de Fuca.

The helicopter carried Julie and her parents to a small private airport near the naval base. They boarded Mr. Furniture's private jet and took off for Los Angeles. As they flew, Julie sat quietly and

The Tiger Cruise

stared out the window. She wondered how she could contact David through the navy. She had not taken the time to get his home address or even an email address. *Maybe I can find it on the Internet,* she thought. She finally closed her eyes and tried to get some rest.

Julie's parents kept looking at her sitting in the back seat, wondering what was wrong with her. They glanced at each other, concerned about her and knowing she had something on her mind. They both finally concluded it was the Rack 2 that was on her mind.

Julie was not able to eat any breakfast in the mess hall because she left so hurriedly, but her parents had brought her something. She wasn't hungry, but she had been trained to eat. Playing the piano and concertizing required much energy, but she was careful not to overeat in order to maintain her attractive figure. The navy food had been so good that it had been challenging for her at the Great Lakes Café. She forced herself to eat what her parents brought her—cold toast and orange juice.

There was so much that was left unsaid in her relationship with David—so many negative thoughts and expressions of unkindness that she had made towards him. Maybe their dissimilar career paths would not allow them to ever meet again. Julie felt guilty and desired to ask him for forgiveness. But maybe it was best that they were apart at this time. She needed to concentrate on something else right now.

* * * * *

On the Michigan an early breakfast would start the day, followed by a wedding on the top of the submarine, then a departure ceremony for the Tiger Crew, and finally a welcome-home celebration with their families. Many of the families of the Tiger Crew had flown to Seattle to meet them. Most of the sailors were being given three-day passes, except for a small maintenance and security crew. Almost everyone was in a festive mood.

* * * * *

The Tiger Cruise

The Kimchi had been towed to an undisclosed location, and David was delivered by helicopter back to the Michigan at 8:00 a.m. He was looking forward to seeing and talking to Julie at breakfast. When he walked into the Great Lakes Café, Ginger was there and told him right away that Julie had already departed the Michigan. He was disappointed.

"I'm sorry about that, David," Ginger said in a consoling voice. "Maybe you can find her during your three-day leave."

"That will be impossible," David replied. "She'll be in Los Angeles. She's probably already there since she is scheduled to perform tonight. I'm sure it's the best for her, anyway. She has enough on her plate right now."

David went through the breakfast chow line and piled it on. He was as hungry as he was tired. The table where Ginger was sitting had two empty seats. Warren had come in and was sitting with her.

David sat down with them and said to Warren, "This is going to be a happy day for you two. It will be an answer to prayer."

"I want to thank you for praying for us, David," Warren expressed. "We will continue to pray for you—and Julie—no matter what happens or what paths your careers may take."

"I prayed for both of you just this morning," Ginger said. "I prayed for God's will to be done in both of your lives. You both have very diverse careers. I believe you have been a great influence on Julie. She told me that you are a spiritual model for her. Maybe that's all the good that will come out of this submarine crisis. But that alone will be worth it."

David was surprised to hear Ginger's words and sat quietly eating his breakfast. *Ginger is right,* he thought. *It may not be God's will to continue my love for Julie.* He was not really sure how she felt about him. She never answered his letter, but there hadn't been enough time. He should have written it sooner. Maybe not meeting her this morning was God's doing and His will. But this was his first real love and he had a firm desire to pursue it—and her. He had only three days to find her. It was not enough time. If God wanted him to find Julie and talk to her, He would have to cause it to happen. How could this possibly happen now?

The Tiger Cruise

The captain met with the Tiger Crew in the Great Lakes Café and presented each of them with a certificate as an "Honorary Sailor on the USS Michigan Trident Nuclear Submarine" for their work for the navy. They were also given a card for their wallets showing that they were official members of the sub. He shook each member's hand and thanked each for his service and unique contributions during the ten-day emergency Tiger Cruise. "I assure you this trip will not be soon forgotten, and it will be etched in your memory for years to come. At the same time, I'm quite certain I wish never to repeat this cruise again. Expect your check from the navy within about two weeks."

The brief wedding ceremony for Warren and Ginger Johnson was held as scheduled at 10:00 a.m. on the top of the Michigan. Captain Wagner performed the five-minute ceremony and made some comments about both of them. Their son Jake was with his mom and dad and was probably as happy as anyone on the sub. David was also in attendance. Julie had also been invited and was noticeably absent. The bride and groom would need to be legally remarried in the state of Michigan later; but for now, this Michigan ceremony would do.

Most of the families and their Tiger Crew sailors met in the Banger Naval Base community room after watching them emerge from the Michigan's top hatch. The news media were not present as the Navy would not permit them through the main gate. Many photos were taken, and Dave Simmons was busy attempting to organize a five-year reunion of this same Tiger Crew.

The Johnson family—Warren, Ginger, and Jake—were busy making plans for their return to Michigan. Jake gave a personal invitation to Captain Wagner to fish on Lake Michigan sometime in the future.

Chapter 12

Captain Wagner and David happened to meet as they were walking away from the Michigan dock toward the parking lot. "What are your plans for the next three days, David?" The captain asked.

"I would like to find Julie," David answered. "I'm sure she's gone to Los Angeles for her concert tonight. So that's out. I never got to say goodbye to her. Maybe I'll just go to my apartment in Silverdale and watch television all weekend."

The captain quickly extended his arm, stopping David abruptly. "I have an idea, David. If you have no plans, why don't you go to her concert tonight?"

"How would I manage that?" David asked. "That would be impossible."

The captain put his arm around David's shoulder and said, "I'm on my way to the airport to catch a plane for Los Angeles to attend a navy conference. If you put on your white uniform, I'll get you on that plane and we'll take you with us."

David stood still with his mouth open. Was this a chance meeting with the captain or was it God's doing? David was sure it was God opening up a door once again. He may get to see Julie and hear her perform on the piano after all! He grabbed the captain's hand and shook it vigorously. David might have given the captain a hug were it not professionally unacceptable.

David raced to his apartment. Within thirty minutes he was cleaned up and in his white uniform and shiny black shoes. He then drove back to the small airport close to the naval base where he met up with Captain Wagner.

The Tiger Cruise

David, Captain Wagner, and six other navy officers were airborne by noon. The captain informed the other officers that David was traveling to Los Angeles on an emergency. No mention was made of his role in the Lost Sub Crisis. The real reason for the trip—that David wanted to see Julie perform at the Hollywood Bowl—was also kept from the other officers. To some degree it was an emergency.

* * * * *

Julie and her parents had taken Mr. Furniture's private plane to Los Angeles. They arrived at the rehearsal hall in time for Julie to work on entrances and to run through the complete Rachmaninoff a couple of times. Her parents couldn't believe the physical endurance demonstrated by their daughter after her isolation on a submarine in the ocean for ten days without practicing on a piano. They couldn't understand it but accepted it without any questions.

* * * * *

In the air David let his imagination run wild. *What does the future hold for my life with Julie?* he asked himself. *How can our careers eventually converge after my naval service and her concert-playing years are finished? Is her piano talent first-rate?* David had never heard her perform. He had only watched her fingers, hands, and arms move. *What will I do after the Navy?*

He began to answer his own questions. Maybe both of them could become teachers in the same college—Julie in music and piano, and David in physical education. But that would mean further education for both of them. His thoughts would start to carry him away, but then the differences in their religion and spiritual philosophies brought him back to earth. He finally came back to reality and decided to take one step at a time. Once the aircraft landed, David needed to get from the airport to the Hollywood Bowl, and then he needed to obtain a ticket to a sold-out concert. That was worry enough for right now.

They soon arrived at a small military airport near Los Angeles. "Follow me," the captain said to David. They went to the parking

The Tiger Cruise

area where two military cars were waiting. The captain went to the front car and told the driver, "Take this sailor to the Hollywood Bowl as quickly as you can."

David was once again speechless. He figured he would need to somehow find his own way to where Julie was to perform—probably hitchhike.

As David was about to enter the car, the captain handed him a note. It was Julie's home phone number, address and email address that she had given him the night before.

David jumped into the car and soon was on his way to the Hollywood Bowl. He had never been in Los Angeles. He had only heard of this outdoor performance arena. His grandfather had left him records of works by orchestras who had performed in the Bowl.

At the ticket counter, a sign indicated that the concert was sold out. "It's been sold out ever since the news came out that the scheduled piano player was on that submarine. Hey, wait a minute," remarked one of the ticket sales people. "Since you're military, I have a ticket here for you. It's not a very good seat but it's a ticket. Someone couldn't make the concert tonight but left it here for anyone who might be in the military." David grabbed the ticket and thanked the man before heading for the bathroom. He had been drinking too much coffee on the flight from Silverdale to Los Angeles.

Just as he walked out of the bathroom, he could hear the orchestra warming up. David didn't know what the orchestra was playing, other than the Rack 2. Wanting to find a better seat, he managed to walk past the person taking tickets and made his way down to the box seats. He spotted one right in front that had an empty chair. A family was seated in the box—a husband, his wife, and two young children. They were just finishing their box lunch. He walked up to them and boldly asked, "Excuse me. May I sit in this empty seat? I just arrived and found out that the tickets are all sold out."

Surprised by the request of the sailor the father said, "You may ... and we even have some food to share." The two children were excited to have a real sailor sit with them. David accepted their offer of food and proceeded to partake of the lunch.

* * * * *

The Tiger Cruise

The conductor for the concert was Sir LeRoy Wheeler, the British maestro who was seventy-one years old. He was reported to be in poor health and was about to retire. It seemed rather odd that he would be matched with such a young soloist as Julie for this concert. There couldn't have been a more diverse age difference. Maybe it was a selling point for tickets.

When he initially came on stage and walked to the podium, David noticed Maestro Wheeler was very pale and was walking a little unsteadily. David had seen this pallor on the faces of his fellow sailors many times onboard the Michigan. They had gotten seasick or had eaten some bad food in a restaurant at some port.

The first work on the program was Mikhail Glinka's Overture to "Russlan and Ludmilla." David noticed Maestro Wheeler seemed to lose his place a couple times. The orchestra players seated around the podium showed concern on their faces and with glances to each other. This particular overture was usually played at a very fast tempo, but it seemed this maestro was trying to set the world's record.

When the overture was completed, there was a short break of about ten minutes. This allowed latecomers to be seated and the Steinway piano to be brought out and placed in the front center of the stage. David happened to notice the morning newspaper protruding out of the young family's picnic basket. A photo of the Michigan was partially showing, along with a photo of Captain Wagner. David looked at it for a moment then looked at the wife and saw that she had noticed him glancing at the newspaper. She immediately connected the Michigan with the sailor sitting in their box with them. "Were you on the Michigan?" she slowly asked.

"Yes I was, ma'am," David answered politely. "We just surfaced this morning, and I just arrived from Washington a short while ago."

"You had quite a trip, didn't you?" she asked.

"Yes we did, ma'am," he answered again.

"Our piano player tonight was on the Michigan, wasn't she?" the woman continued her inquiry. "Did you get to meet her?"

"Yes I did, ma'am," David again answered.

It was now time for the Rachmaninoff. David's heart was beating as he anticipated Julie's appearance on stage. He wondered

The Tiger Cruise

what she would be wearing. He had seen her only in the clothes she was wearing when she boarded the Michigan and the navy clothes provided to her. David could only imagine how beautiful she would be in a dress—probably a long formal gown. What color would it be and how would she have her long black hair fixed?

The moment arrived. The stage door opened, and Julie walked out dressed in a full-length satin white gown that went almost all the way to the floor. There would be just enough room for her to manipulate the piano peddles with her long legs and black shoes. Her hair was tied together neatly on her head, just like she had it on the Michigan. David knew she had long black hair, but he had never seen it long.

Maestro Wheeler followed her. There was a prolonged standing applause for Julie. The news coverage had done its job. David's heart was beating fast in anticipation of what he expected next—his favorite piano concerto.

Soon the applause stopped and the conductor took his place on the podium. David knew the history of this concerto very well. It was one of the most difficult to play, technically. Rachmaninoff had composed it three years after a disastrous performance of his first symphony, as reported by the music critics, which caused him to sink into a state of depression. After seeking some professional counseling he snapped back to his old self and wrote this most popular of all his works, the Concerto Number 2 for piano and orchestra. He dedicated the concerto to the professional who had counseled him—a hypnotist doctor.

Julie sat down at the piano. She turned her head and panned the audience. She saw her parents. Her head suddenly stopped and her eyes were fixed on someone. By chance she spotted a sailor in a white uniform. The box where he was sitting was close and clearly visible. *Is that David dressed in his Navy uniform?* she wondered. She gave a quick smile and closed her eyes for five seconds. That wasn't David. It couldn't be. He was still in the state of Washington. He wouldn't be sitting in the boxes anyway. *The smile was for some other sailor,* Julie thought. She opened her eyes to the piano keys. It was time for the concerto to begin.

The Tiger Cruise

David was worried about the conductor. The color of his face had worsened and indicated he was about to have a stroke or a heart attack or at least pass out. He had seen it several times aboard the submarine. "Once you see it, get ready to catch them," was how he had been trained, "especially if you're on top of the submarine in the middle of the Pacific Ocean." Maybe the conductor was just old and there was nothing to worry about. *But he doesn't look well at all,* David concluded.

The conductor took his cue from Julie. She nodded her head that she was ready to begin the "moderato movement." When she came in with the first eight unaccompanied chords, tears suddenly welled up in David's eyes. He loved this concerto and had it memorized in his mind, often conducting it while listening to it at night. He had no baton. Besides, there was not enough room for him to use a baton in his small bunk by the nuclear silos. The bunks on the Michigan were not much bigger than the inside of a coffin.

His hostess noticed David's tears and sensed the emotion David was experiencing. She took his hand and held it until the tears had stopped.

Julie's playing was superb. David's eyes were glued to the keyboard, which was clearly visible from where he was sitting. Her long arms and fingers produced both the power and tenderness that were required in the concerto.

Toward the end of the first movement, the conductor began to lose his tempo. Julie and the orchestra immediately noticed what was happening, as did the audience. Julie was now ignoring the conductor and leading the orchestra with her playing. Her playing was outstanding, in spite of the circumstances.

Finally, just as the first movement ended, the conductor slumped over and rolled onto the floor. There was a low roar from the audience. The concertmaster quickly set his violin on his chair and rushed to the conductor's side. The principal cellist and some of the stage hands rushed to the podium as if they also had been expecting this to happen.

David wondered what was going to happen now. Something told him to check it out. He stood up, excused himself from his hosts, and ran toward where he thought the backstage door was located. As

The Tiger Cruise

he was running, he began hearing the sirens of emergency vehicles in the distance. He walked up to the stage door leading into where the orchestra and Julie were seated. Perhaps because he had a military uniform on, no one seemed to question him having the right to be there.

The subdued conversations of the people in charge centered on whether they were even going to continue the concert. Because of the uncertainty of Julie's availability as the featured artist for this concert, no one had secured an alternate conductor. They did have a backup pianist, but not a backup conductor. They may have been able to find someone on an hour's notice, but could they find someone in ten minutes who would be familiar with the Rack 2? Surely someone within the orchestra could take up the baton, but no one seemed willing to volunteer. Someone had not done their job.

It was no more than a few minutes and the ambulance had taken the conductor away. The orchestra and Julie had remained seated so the emergency personnel could do their job. Everyone in attendance assumed a replacement conductor would soon walk out and continue with the second movement. The audience commotion grew as the seconds passed.

David overheard two officials whispering to each other about what they were going to tell the audience when one of them walked out to make the cancellation announcement. They were quietly arguing who was going to do it.

Meanwhile, Julie was about to walk off the stage to ask if the concerto was going to be continued. David decided to make sure Julie's special night was not ruined. He was about to take the biggest risk of his life. It would take all the courage he could muster—even more than diving off the Michigan and entering the North Korean submarine and risking getting his head blown off. He knew he could be arrested or, even worse, disciplined by the Navy. He needed to act quickly and decisively. Just like he had saved Ginger out of the ocean, he was now about to save Julie's big performance.

He went to the stage door and opened it. No one tried to stop him, and he silently prayed as he walked through the orchestra toward the podium, *Lord, help me! Give me guts! Direct me.* The audience started to quiet down, so that by the time he reached to podium it

The Tiger Cruise

was almost completely silent. The audience was wondering what a young sailor was doing on stage. Maybe the young sailor was the replacement conductor dressed in a navy uniform.

Julie didn't see David until he was standing by the podium. She was sitting and looking at the audience where her mother and father were sitting. David stepped onto the podium and bowed to the audience. They slowly began to applaud. Julie suddenly realized what was going on and her heart started to pound. At first she just sat on the piano bench stunned, not recognizing David in his white navy uniform. Then she came alive and quickly covered her eyes. *What is David going to do?* she thought. *Why is he here? How did he get here?*

David needed to let everyone know that there was a legitimate connection between Julie and him and that his presence was to make certain that the Rack 2 went on. It may just keep the authorities, who surely would be alerted by this time, from rushing onto the stage and dragging him off to jail for disturbing the peace.

David stepped off of the podium and walked toward Julie. She stood up to meet him and put out her hand. *Shaking hands won't be enough,* David thought. He gently pulled her to him, embraced her, and gave her an unexpected kiss. The audience immediately broke out with loud applause, then cheering. It confirmed their suspicion that these two young people must have met on the just completed cruise on the USS Michigan, as was reported in every newspaper in the English-speaking world. They held their embrace as the audience increased the volume of their ovation.

As David finally released her from his embrace, Julie whispered in his ear, "Now what?"

David whispered back in Julie's ear, "Rack 2—second movement."

Now it was time for the second and third movements. Before any officials could summon any authorities, David had to start. He picked up the baton from the floor and placed it on the conductor's stand. He didn't need it.

He raised his hands and said quietly, but with a noticeable movement of his mouth, "Second movement." The strings raised their instruments and bows, not having any idea if the sailor had any experience in conducting or if he even knew what he was doing. But they had no choice. If he could start them together in the correct tempo, they were sure they could follow each other and the piano. David had the same thought.

It began. The tempo of the "adagio" movement was just as it was in the recording David had listened to on his headphones and conducted hundreds times while lying in his bunk aboard the USS Michigan. The famous romantic nocturnal theme of the slow movement had begun, and the concert was continuing. As the theme was passed from the strings to the flute and then to the clarinet David's memory of his time on the Michigan with Julie was brought into his mind with passion.

Within the first few bars of the movement, Julie was a flood of tears. All day long she kept thinking she may never see David again. Now he was conducting her in a piano concerto. *This has to be a dream,* she thought. *This was not by chance—it was orchestrated.*

David could only imagine what Julie was thinking. What was happening was almost a dream. They couldn't have written a more bizarre scenario: An enlisted sailor and a world-class pianist spend ten days on a nuclear submarine, and the day they surface they are performing together at the Hollywood Bowl.

The conductor passing out and David's sudden appearance was more than Julie's emotions could handle. Her eyes were so wet that it was difficult to focus on the piano keys, as well as that special person conducting. She just shut her eyes tight. She knew the music.

Julie was thinking of something else as she continued to play the second movement. David and Ginger had convinced her that she needed a change in her spiritual life. Up until this point in her young life, she had lived only for herself. God had given her a talent, and she needed to give Him something in return. Julie knew what it was. What God really wanted from her was her heart, soul and life. He wanted to be the center of her existence. She also knew that if she was ever to have any lasting relationship with David, she would first need to give up her heart to the Creator of the universe. The decision was made as she continued the second movement.

David thought of all the events that had happened leading up to this point. Was it by chance? No way. This was meant to be.

The Tiger Cruise

The notes flowed from the piano like clear water over a waterfall. David's eyes were shifting between the orchestra and Julie through the entire movement. Whatever flaws were in David's conducting were immediately forgiven by the orchestra and the audience.

At the completion of the second movement, David stepped off the podium. He decided to do something that was unprecedented. He walked to where Julie was sitting at the piano and stood behind her. Placing his hands on Julie's shoulders, he began to rub them in the same manner he had on the Michigan a few days earlier. It was a back rub that was more erotic than therapeutic. But to Julie it was a healing experience, and it helped to release all of the tension within her. Her tears had stopped. The audience sat absolutely quiet. This was a first. It was a fitting interlude after concluding the second movement of the most romantic of all piano concertos.

The audience started applauding as David walked back to the podium. The applause accelerated to a standing ovation. Julie was now ready to play the difficult "allegro" movement.

The final movement was played with all of the passion and virtuosity that Julie could gather. The difficult passages that she had practiced on her felt piano came off without a mistake. It was perfect. David made a few mistakes, but once again the crowd forgave him. The piano and orchestra played together as if they had fallen in love with each other, answering one another passionately. At the point where the final passage began, David and Julie looked at each other to ensure they came in together.

Julie positioned herself back from the piano a few inches. She was preparing to attack the keys with great gusto. The audience was noticeably also preparing themselves. They all knew what was coming.

All of a sudden, Julie reached up and pulled out whatever was keeping her hair on top of her head, and it all fell down. David looked and saw her long black hair for the first time. It was beautiful, and David felt certain Julie was sending a message to him.

Immediately after the final four Rachmaninoff signature notes were played, Julie suddenly jumped up from her bench and David almost leaped from the podium. They grabbed each other and embraced. The audience went wild—another standing ovation.

The Tiger Cruise

"You were great, Julie," David said passionately, "I love you."

"I love you too, David," Julie said in returned, "And have I got a surprise for you!"

David suddenly looked puzzled.

The multiple curtain calls prompted David to suggest that Julie play an encore. She announced her choice. "I wish to play for you the Rachmaninoff Prelude Opus 23, No. 5."

Julie played it flawlessly and the audience applauded.

It was now intermission.

Backstage Julie's parents were waiting for both of them. Even before the introductions, Mrs. Furniture grabbed David and gave him a prolonged hug that rivaled Julie's hug a few moments earlier. "Thank you for what you did tonight. Thank you from Julie, from us, from the audience, from the orchestra," she said. "It was unbelievable." She stepped back from David. "Now, Julie, please introduce your parents to this tall, good-looking sailor. Who in the world are you?"

Julie couldn't wait to make the introduction. "This is David Cordell," Julie said, "the man that I learned to respect and admire on the USS Michigan submarine during the past ten days. He is also the one who provided me with a felt piano, a CD of the Rack 2, a CD player, and a set of headphones."

David didn't look surprised at Julie's comment about the felt piano keyboard. He suspected that she knew.

"Let's all go have something to eat. I'm hungry," Mr. Furniture suggested. "I imagine you kids would appreciate some good cooking after being on that sub for ten days, wouldn't you?"

David and Julie quickly looked at each other and just smiled. *They don't know what good food is,* they both thought together.

"If you want some good food," Julie said to her parents, "then you need to get on a United States Navy submarine. It's the best cooking in the world."

"Hey, who is conducting the remaining piece on the program?" David asked Julie's parents.

"I believe they just recruited another sailor," her father answered with a hearty laugh.

The Tiger Cruise

All of a sudden and out of the blue, a very familiar face to David and Julie appeared. It was Captain Wagner. "Great concert, Julie," the captain complimented. He was done with his high-level meeting and wanted to make it to her concert. Captain Wagner gave Julie a hug and David a grand handshake. David then came to attention and saluted the captain. The captain returned the sulute.

David and Julie introduced the captain to her parents. "This is the best submarine commander in the world," Julie said to her parents.

David and Julie took a taxi to a restaurant her parents had suggested. David needed to talk with Julie alone, and she couldn't wait to talk to David.

David spoke first. "Julie, I want to tell you how I feel about you." She smiled at David. She knew what was coming and was prepared for it. "First of all, I am in love with you and care about you very much."

Julie couldn't wait for him to continue, so she interrupted. "Well, I love you too, David. My parents want you to join us for the next two days here in Los Angeles."

David all of sudden changed his face to a serious stare. He took Julie's hand, looked directly into her eyes and said, "Julie, we need to be careful, I'm not sure you and I can continue our relationship beyond tonight."

Julie once again interrupted him. "I know exactly what you're going to say. You're going to tell me you and I are not on the same page spiritually as well as professionally. Am I correct?"

"Well, yes, Julie," David answered with a sudden look of sadness.

"Well," Julie continued, "you're half right and half wrong. I am a piano player with a bright future, and you are a navy man with a bright future in whatever you decide to do. But you know what? You and I should let God work that out."

David sat quietly with a puzzled look on his face, trying to figure out where Julie's train of thought was leading. Suddenly, his expression turned to a happy one; he knew what had happened to her.

"Tonight when you were busy conducting the second movement of the Rack 2, I was doing something else. At the beginning, you

The Tiger Cruise

and I were on different pages spiritually. During that second movement, I turned the page and moved to be with God and you. Why do you think I was crying so much? I can't even remember playing the notes. One of God's angels must have been playing the piano keys ... or at least guiding my hands."

David closed his eyes for a moment and then opened them. "You know, I had a feeling something like that was happening."

"So, where do we go from here?" Julie asked David.

He was all set with the answer. "I go back on the Michigan submarine or wherever the Navy sends me, and you keep playing the piano for audiences wherever they ask for you or wherever your agent sends you. I will write letters and emails to you, you will write letters and emails to me. We'll pray for each other and for us. Then we'll see what happens and where God leads us."

"I think He may lead us back to each other," Julie said softly.

"I am sure that is where it will lead," David replied.

"And for the next two days we'll spend time with my parents so they and I can get to know you better," Julie responded.

"It will be fun," David answered, "and they'll be our chaperones." Then in all seriousness he said to her, "By the way, Julie, God's angel sounded pretty good in that second movement ... almost as good as you."

"Maybe," she responded.

They both grinned.

The End

Breinigsville, PA USA
18 September 2009
224326BV00002B/2/P